P. Martin Ostrander's
Dangerous Four Series

P. Martin Ostrander's
Dangerous Four Series

✦

Book #2: The Deadly Crash

P. Martin Ostrander

iUniverse, Inc.

New York   Bloomington

P. Martin Ostrander's Dangerous Four Series
Book #2: The Deadly Crash

*This is a work of fiction. All of the characters, names, incidents, organizations, and dialogue in
this novel are either the products of the author's imagination or are used fictitiously.*

iUniverse books may be ordered through booksellers or by contacting:

iUniverse
1663 Liberty Drive
Bloomington, IN 47403
www.iuniverse.com
1-800-Authors (1-800-288-4677)

ISBN: 978-1-4401-1811-1 (pbk)
ISBN: 978-1-4401-1812-8 (ebk)

Printed in the United States of America

iUniverse rev. date: 3/4/2009

For Anyone Who Likes Music

CHAPTER 1

Jamie sat across from Sarah at their usual lunch table Monday at school. She had been debating telling Sarah what happened between her and Jake during the party for a while now, and she'd finally decided to come clean. She took another bite of her burger and eagerly awaited Sarah's response.

"OK, let me get this straight. You had Jake all alone in your room, and all you could do was tell him you had Left-y's autograph? Why didn't you tell him the truth?"

"I did; I really did get Left-y's autograph. You even saw it."

"That's not what I meant. Why didn't you tell Jake how you really feel about him?"

"I … I just couldn't do it. What if he laughed at me? I don't think I could take it."

"Jamie, listen to me. You've got to tell him. If you don't, eventually someone else will."

"Who, like you?"

"No, not me, but someone."

"Thanks a lot, Sarah."

"I meant to help."

"I know."

"Look, I've known Jake longer than you have. He won't laugh at you. Just tell him. Trust me on this."

Jamie sighed and took another bite of her burger. "I hope so."

Jake picked a few black olives off his cold pizza. He hated those things. He didn't like leftover pizza either, but since he was still riding high from The Costumed Battle of the Bands, he ate it anyway. He had never been more nervous about performing than that night. When the audience cheered, though, and The Dangerous Four were announced as the winners, he knew the four of them had something special and couldn't wait to see what else they would do.

"Our next practice is going to be tonight," he said eagerly.

"Already?" Craig asked. "I thought we were going to take a break. It's only been a few days."

"We don't want to get lazy. We made the front page of the paper and we've been on TV. People are starting to notice us. Craig, you even said it was totally awesome. You don't want to lose that."

"No, but I don't want to have to practice all the time either. I didn't like it. None of us did."

"No, we didn't," Jake said, as he thought for a moment. "How about we only practice for a half hour—eleven-thirty till midnight, like we used to?"

"I can do that," Craig said.

The others agreed.

"We'll meet then," Jake said as the bell rang and the four of them went back to class.

That night, Jamie tossed and turned in her bed forever, but she just could not get to sleep. Counting sheep didn't help much either.

She rolled over and fell out of bed. Thunk! She got back up a little dazed and looked at her clock radio—just past eleven-thirty. That's when she remembered the music. She hadn't heard it for a while and hoped she would tonight. She quickly got back on her bed and opened her window. A light, cool breeze hit her and made her shiver. The air seemed to be getting colder every day. Soon it would be too cold to open her window, so she had to find out about the music, and soon.

As she stared out at the open field and dark clear sky, her mind began to wander, and her thoughts turned to Jake. She had to tell him how she felt, but not with everyone there. She had to get him alone somehow.

Her thoughts were interrupted by the sound of the sweet music. It was soft at first but grew louder and louder until she could hear it quite clearly. She loved it so much. If only she knew where it was coming from. Jamie pounded her fist on the windowsill. She couldn't stand it anymore. She had to find out. Jamie looked out her window and saw that their shed was right below. The roof couldn't be more than a few feet away, and an old stepladder was leaning against the wall. Jamie quickly and quietly got dressed and lowered herself out the window and onto the shed.

She couldn't believe she was doing this in the middle of the night, as she walked out of her backyard and into the field. Why hadn't she brought a coat? It was early November, but it felt like December. Her radio had said it was a nice fifty-five degrees out, but it felt a lot colder. The field was easy to walk through, for most of the plants had been cut down or were dying because winter was coming. All was going fine, when all of a sudden …

Squish!

Jamie made a face as she had no idea what she had just stepped in.

She scraped a piece of whatever it was off with her finger and smelled it, discovering to her relief that it was just mud. Relieved, she went on.

Jamie continued to walk farther and farther out into the field, her house no longer in view. She hadn't heard the music for a while and wasn't sure she was going in the right direction. There were no lights shining from town, and she had forgotten to get a flashlight. Now she wasn't sure where to go. As she sat down on an old log, she buried her head in her hands and tried to hold back her tears. She couldn't believe it, but it was true. She was lost. How in the world could this have happened? She'd been out in the field tons of times but never this far and never this late before. She was about to burst into a full sob when she heard it. She jerked her head up and listened as hard as she could. There it was—the same amazing music she'd heard in her room so many nights before, except this time it was much louder. She jumped up and wiped her eyes. She thought hard and decided that the music was coming from in front of her. She gathered her strength and began to walk toward the sounds. After a couple of steps, she began to jog, and then broke into a full-out run. The music was getting louder by the second. She knew she was getting close.

◆   ◆   ◆

Left-y sang the chorus to "Liking You" as he strummed to the rhythm. He stopped singing and backed up Rousey's guitar solo. After a few notes, all of them stopped playing.

"Well, we're to the end, and still no ending."

"That's what you think, Left-y. How's this for an ending?" Rousey asked as he jammed a few notes on his guitar. He hit a sour pitch, and everyone squirmed.

Drummey covered his ears. "What the heck was that?"

"Only the greatest ending ever played."

"Yeah, maybe if you're deaf."

"Hey, shut up, Drummey. You can't do any better."

"At least I can tell if a note is sour or not."

"Ah, what do you know? Left-y, you thought it was good, didn't you?"

"Uh, well, it could use a little work."

"Yeah," Rightey added. "Like the whole thing!"

Drummey burst out laughing. He laughed so hard, he fell off his stool, and he still kept laughing. Left-y and Rightey began to laugh at Drummey, and finally Rousey joined in. After a while, it seemed as though they'd never stop, but finally Left-y got a hold of himself.

"OK, guys," he said as he gulped in air. "We've got to stop. I think I'm going to puke."

"Yeah, me too," Drummey said as he got back on his stool and picked up his drumsticks.

"What are we going to do?" Rousey asked.

"How about we forget 'Liking You' for now and try 'Our Awesome Stash.'"

"Good idea, Left-y. I like that song. It actually has an ending."

"All right, you guys ready?"

"Ready."

"Let's make some tunes!"

Jamie ran as fast as her legs would let her. She ran and ran, and then she stopped dead in her tracks. She had to look twice to make sure she was seeing it right. What she saw was a small, old shack off in the distance. There was a light on, and people were inside. She knew the music was coming from there. She'd found it! Jamie was so excited she almost forgot to move her legs and nearly fell over but caught herself in time. She ran full speed to the shack, but was careful not to be in the light of the door so whoever was in there wouldn't see her. As she slowly walked around the shack, she noticed a few bikes against one of the walls.

Jamie figured it must be a boys' clubhouse as she continued to creep around to the wall with the window. She didn't have to creep much, though. The music drowned out her footsteps. She got to the wall and looked at the window. It was too high for her to peek in—or was it? She noticed a couple of old crates underneath. They looked sturdy enough, so she decided to try them. She carefully stepped up onto them and peeked in.

Jamie had no idea what to make of the whole scene. There was Jake, Nick, Craig, and Ryan—all with musical instruments and playing a song. She recognized the melody at once. It was "Our Awesome Stash." What in the world were the four of them doing? The only group who could play that song was The ... No, it couldn't be, but it seemed to be. Jamie couldn't believe it!

She watched in awe as each of the boys did his own part and played beautifully together. She wanted to keep watching, but her leg was cramping up. She shifted her weight but the wrong way, and the crates gave way. She came crashing down with a loud crack as the wood broke, and she fell to the ground.

Left-y, along with the others, suddenly stopped playing, frozen in the silence with fear—fear that what they'd heard was true. They tried to push it out of their minds, but it didn't work. They couldn't ignore it.

Finally, Rousey spoke: "Did you guys hear that?"

They all nodded.

"What the heck was that?"

At first, none of them could answer, but after a few seconds, Left-y finally found the courage to speak: "Someone knows."

CHAPTER 2

"What do you mean someone knows?" Rousey demanded as he ripped off his sunglasses and glared at Left-y.

"I mean someone knows we're here."

"What are you talking about? Maybe it was the wind."

"I don't think so."

"Hey guys," Drummey interrupted, "why don't we go out and see. If someone really is here, let's find out who."

They dropped their instruments and ran outside, only to find nothing. Then they ran around to the back, but still nothing. Finally, they ran to the sidewall with the window, just in time to see someone get up and attempt to run away, but whoever it was tripped over something and fell.

"Ouch! That hurt!"

"It's a girl's voice," Rousey shouted. "After her!"

They easily caught up with her and had her by the arms, but no one could see who she was.

"Let's get her inside with the light," Left-y said.

Together, all four of them dragged the girl into the clubhouse and nearly dropped her to the ground.

"Jamie!" all of them screamed at once. "What the heck are you doing here?"

"What am I doing here? What are you four doing here? I can't believe you guys, sneaking out late at night like this to some old shack in the middle of nowhere. Do your parents know?"

"No, and don't you …"

"Don't worry, I won't tell. My parents would freak out too if they knew I'd snuck out. I'm not even a teenager yet. What's worse is you're impersonating The Dangerous Four. How dare you! I'm good friends with them, and once they hear about this, you'll really get it!"

"Oh no, you can't do that," Rousey begged her in the most sarcastic way possible. "You can't tell any of them, especially Rousey; I hear he's real tough. Please promise me you won't tell them."

"Maybe I will, Craig, and maybe I won't."

Left-y suddenly realized she didn't know it was them. She didn't know they were The Dangerous Four.

"What are you guys doing out here anyway?"

"Oh, nothing really, just practicing."

"Well, as much as I hate to admit it, you guys did sound pretty good, almost as good as The Dangerous Four. Hey, that looks just like Drummey's drum set, and that's Left-y's guitar, and … wait a minute; what are you doing with their instruments?"

"You're joking, right?" Rousey asked. "How stupid are you?"

"At least I'm smart enough to know when to wear sunglasses," she said as she bent over and plucked one of Rousey's guitar strings.

"Hey! Hands off my guitar!"

Jamie looked at him funny.

"What do you mean hands off your guitar? This is Rousey's, unless that means …"

"You got it, girl," Rousey said, as the four of them stood together. "We are The Dangerous Four."

"No way, but you are. This is awesome!"

"Yeah, I guess it is pretty cool to be us, and you thought we were just a bunch of dorks."

"No, Craig, she just thought you were a dork. Now, can you guess our stage names?"

"Well, Jake, I know you're left-handed, so you're Left-y. I saw Ryan on the drums, so he's Drummey. Craig got all mad when I plucked Rousey's guitar, so he's Rousey, and that leaves Nick, who has to be Rightey. How'd I do?"

"Perfect, you really know us."

"I'm your biggest fan, Left-y."

"Then I guess you know how we became a group."

"Yeah, I've followed you guys since your first performance."

"Wow," Rightey said as he picked up his bass and plucked it a couple of times. "Then you know everything about us."

"Well, not quite everything. I didn't know who you guys were until tonight."

"Now you do," Left-y said as he checked his watch. "It's late. Let's clean up," Jamie headed for the door, and Left-y called after her, "Oh, Jamie."

"Yeah?"

"Don't tell anyone about tonight, OK?"

"Don't worry; I won't tell. Besides, would anyone believe me?"

"I guess you're right. You'd better get back before your parents realize you're gone."

"I suppose I should. Hey, could I come to one of your practices?

"And do what?" Left-y asked.

"Watch you guys."

Left-y thought for a moment. "I guess you could …"

"We'll let you know," Rousey interrupted.

Jamie looked at him funny. "OK, I'll see you at school. Bye, Jakey!"

He gave her a quick wave, and she left.

Once they were sure she was gone, Rousey exploded. "This is awful!" he cried as he sat down and put his head in his hands. "I knew this was going to happen sooner or later, and a girl. Of all people, a girl had to find out. Well, kiss the masks good-bye. No more sneaking around. No more fun. We're done for!"

"Rousey, I think you're overreacting. She said she wouldn't tell anyone."

"Left-y, this is Jamie we're talking about here. She's got the biggest mouth in school. She'll tell everyone she knows, and you were going to invite her back to watch us practice."

"If she tries to tell anyone, who would believe her? No one knows our true identities; why would anyone believe it's us? Besides, why couldn't she watch us practice? It wouldn't hurt anything."

"Left-y does have a good point," Drummey said as he finished picking up his drums. Rousey looked at Left-y and frowned.

"You're just saying that because you like her."

Left-y was stunned. He had told Rousey that Jamie did not have a crush on him like they all thought. He didn't hate her like Rousey did, but he didn't like her like her either.

"I just don't think it's a big deal," he replied.

"I don't like it," Rousey said as he got up to leave. "I don't like this."

Jamie turned over in her bed and nearly fell out again. She tried to sleep, but her mind was going crazy. She checked her clock—1:30.

The harder she tried to fall asleep, the more awake she became. She was just too excited. Her thoughts kept going back to Jake, or maybe it was Left-y she thought about. What difference did it make? They were the same person. She couldn't wait to see him at school the next day. They could hint about things that happened the night before, and no one would have a clue that anything was going on. The night had been so much fun. There they were—four rock stars and their biggest fan, and yet just five kids who had snuck out in the middle of the night and had a secret club meeting. She didn't know what to make of it. All she knew was that she knew a secret—a really, really, big secret, and she couldn't tell anyone, not even Sarah. Who would believe her? Would Sarah even believe her?

She also wondered how knowing this would change things with her and them. Maybe she could travel with them. No. That wouldn't work. She'd just be in the way. She thought about The Dangerous Four some more until her mind relaxed then realized she was tired. She figured she'd talk to them tomorrow. Jamie's thoughts drifted back to the music of The Dangerous Four. While their songs played in her head, she finally fell asleep.

◆   ◆   ◆

Left-y had spent the next few days trying to convince Rousey to let Jamie come to one of their practices. Left-y knew Jamie a lot better than Rousey did and believed she would keep their secret. Rousey had finally given in, and The Dangerous Four were eagerly waiting in the clubhouse for Jamie.

Left-y got up from his chair and began to pace. "I can't believe the news is still taking about us."

"Me neither," Rousey agreed. "We're famous now."

"We're not quite famous," Drummey said as he spun his drumstick, "but we're way more popular than I ever thought we'd be."

"That's for sure. I think it's great."

"Yeah, Rightey, it is great," Left-y said as he checked his watch again.

"She's not going to show up, Left-y. She's already ten minutes late."

"She'll be here, Rousey. She'll be here."

"I knew having a girl in this was a bad idea. Let's just start without her."

"The heck you will," Jamie announced, as she appeared in the doorway to make her dramatic, and slightly late, appearance. She stepped into the light, and her face revealed the look of extreme tiredness. She wore a red and white windbreaker with jeans and had her hair pulled back in a ponytail.

"Well, look who finally showed up."

"Rousey, give her a break. She came, didn't she?"

"Thank you, Left-y, but I can handle this," Jamie said as she walked over to Rousey and got right in his face.

"You have no idea how hard this place is to find. I'm amazed I found it the other night, and my parents would never get to bed. I thought they were going to be up all night. And another thing ..."

"OK, OK, I get the point. You were held up, sorry!"

"Thank you. Now that I'm here, you guys can practice."

"Yes, we can," Left-y said.

"So, what are we going to do?" Rightey asked.

"Hmmm, hey I know! We could play 'Liking You' for Jamie and see if she could come up with an ending to it."

"Left-y, that's a stupid idea," Rousey said as he put his sunglasses on. "Jamie has no musical talent. How could she write an ending to something as important as this—oh, no offense, of course."

"I'm not offended, Rousey. It's true. I'm not very good with music stuff. I wouldn't know what to do."

"Well, would you at least like to hear it?"

"I would love to, Jakey."

"Great, and stop calling me that, will you?"

"Uh, no," Jamie said as she sat back in a wooden chair, and they began to play.

The Dangerous Four had never sounded so good. She couldn't believe how great the song was. All the notes seemed to flow together perfectly. The coolest thing was she was listening to a song as it was being made. No one would get to hear it for quite a while, but she was hearing it now.

Jamie was so caught up in the music she almost didn't notice that they had stopped playing. They were at the end, but with no ending. She didn't know what to say.

"That sounded great. You're right, though, it does need an ending; but I have no idea how to finish it. I'm clueless."

"Just like the rest of us," Left-y said sadly. "Thanks for listening to it."

"Are you kidding? I'd always listen to you guys. I love The Dangerous Four."

"Thanks, Jamie," Left-y said. "Why don't we play a few more songs."

They ran through the rest of their songs. After what didn't feel like very long to Jamie, Left-y looked at his watch. "Well, it's after midnight. We might as well quit."

"Yeah, we might as well," added Drummey. "I heard the weather's supposed to be bad out tonight anyway."

The four of them put away their instruments and cleaned up. Jamie walked over to the table where some newspaper articles were laying. "The Dangerous Four Rock the Stage!" and "The Dangerous Four Appear Live for Costumed Battle of the Bands" were a couple of the articles she skimmed over.

They more or less said the same thing. The Dangerous Four gave a great performance, and the audience loved them. Jamie wondered what it was like for them up there—all those people chanting their names and screaming for them, not to mention the lights and cameras. She thought back to when the foursome had headlined their first concert. She had gone with Sarah to see them, and The Dangerous Four had been amazing. She also thought it was amazing that she wanted so badly to be able to unmask them, and now she had. She knew who they were. Maybe they would take her with them when they did concerts. She could help out and maybe even be on stage with them once or twice. Maybe after long enough, she could join them. No, no way could that happen. She wasn't good with music, but what if she practiced? After all, they just weren't born good musicians. All four of them had to start somewhere. She could do that. But would they even let her try?

That was a question that Jamie would have to ask, but not then. It would have to be later. The next meeting, perhaps, or maybe the one after, but sometime soon. Maybe they would understand. Maybe they would let her try. Maybe they would like her. What if they did? What if they let her in? What if she became a member of The Dangerous Four?

CHAPTER 3

It was after midnight in the old clubhouse. Jamie had left a few minutes before, and The Dangerous Four were picking up getting ready to leave. Left-y and Drummey were on one side putting the instruments away, while Rightey and Rousey got them ready. As Rightey was about to walk over to Left-y and Drummey with the last of the cords, Rousey nudged him and whispered:

"Hey, Rightey, did you see the way Jamie was looking at us tonight?"

"Yeah, she looked at us. She was watching us the whole time, big deal."

"No, I mean the way she looked at us, especially at Left-y? She was practically mesmerized by him, and he was a little off tonight. He'd even admit it."

"So Jamie liked to watch Left-y play, so what?"

"So what? I think that girl's got some kind of crush on him."

"I don't think so, Rousey, but even if she did, why should we care? It's not hurting anyone."

"You like being in the band, don't you?"

"Of course I do. I wouldn't be here if I didn't."

"Good, then you can help get rid of Jamie, because if she stays, everything is going to change."

"What are you talking about? How could Jamie change things?"

"That's what girls do. She'll want us to do things her way. She'll convince Left-y first, and once he's on her side, it's all over."

"Rousey, that's stupid. I think your making this a way bigger deal than it is. Left-y would never let that happen. He's too into The Dangerous Four."

"You don't know girls the way I do. They can make boys do strange things. I know everything about them."

"And how many girlfriends have you had?"

"Well none, but that doesn't mean I don't know how they work. Trust me; including Jamie is a bad idea."

"Man, Rousey, you worry too much. We'll always have the band. That's not going to change."

"I hope you're right. I still don't trust her. There's just something about her I don't like. Anyways, I'm getting tired. I'll see you tomorrow at school."

"Bye, Rousey," Rightey said as Rousey walked out into the night.

Rightey shook his head. Sometimes he just didn't know what to make of Rousey. He seemed to make some things such a crisis. There was never any way to know if he was actually telling the truth or not. It wasn't that he was doing it to be mean or anything. Rousey was a nice kid. Rightey liked him; heck everyone did, except for the girls. No girl could stand him. Maybe it was because he was never nice to them, or maybe it was because he wore his sunglasses all the time. Rightey wasn't sure. He went over to help Left-y and Drummey pick up. Left-y had just put the last of the instruments away.

"Hey, Left-y, how come you didn't put your guitar away with everything else?"

"Because," he began in a highly deductive tone, "then my dad would start to wonder where his guitar went. He may not use it, but he would know if it was missing. He'd ask me about it, and I really don't want to have to tell him."

"Ah, I see."

"Hey, where's Rousey?" Drummey asked suddenly.

"He already left."

"That sounds like Rousey; he's never around to help out. Always late, and he takes off early."

"What else did we need him for, Left-y? We've done everything."

"Yeah, I guess you're right. It's just that you two stayed to help, and sometimes I wonder."

"You wonder what?" Drummey asked.

"I don't know. I just wish he'd be more responsible sometimes, more serious about things. Sometimes I wonder if he even takes The Dangerous Four seriously or if he's just in it for fun, and that's all."

Rightey stepped up and looked Left-y straight in the face and said, "Rousey can be confusing sometimes, but one thing I know for sure is that he's serious about the band, about all of us. He's here for the right reasons."

Left-y put his hand on Rightey's shoulder. "Thanks Rightey, you're a good friend, and so are you, Drummey," he said as he walked to the door and gazed out into the night.

"We'll always be friends, no matter what happens," Rightey said as he and Drummey joined him.

For a moment the three of them stared into the night sky, and then Left-y spoke: "Well, I guess there's nothing else to do here. We'd better get going."

"I agree," Drummey said as the three of them left the clubhouse and went home.

Jake's late night up had caused him to oversleep and miss the bus again, so his mom had to give him a ride to school. He got out just in time to avoid a kiss good-bye. He couldn't believe his mom had tried to pull something like that on him. He was the baby of the family, true, but he was eleven years old—most of his friends were still ten—but his mom just didn't understand.

As he approached the end of his class line, he heard a voice call, "Jakey, I saved you a spot up here by me."

He looked and saw Jamie waving him over. He stepped out of line and walked up to her. He was nearly there when he felt a jerk on his back collar, which nearly caused him to choke and stopped him dead in his tracks. He knew exactly who it was.

"And just where do you think you're going?" asked Tone "The Bone" in his big, tough voice.

"Uh, up to Jamie. She waved me up."

"I don't think so, jerk! You're going back to the end of the line where you belong."

"You'd better let me go, or I'll …" Jake couldn't believe he'd just said that.

"You'll what?" Tone said as he glared and snarled at Jake. He took a step toward Jake and pounded his right fist into the palm of his left hand. "Either you get back there now, or I'm going to knock you back—clear back to the end of the line."

Jake took a step back. He knew he was way outmuscled and no match for Tone. He was about to start for the end of the line, but Jamie spoke up: "Leave him alone, Anthony. I said he could be by me. Why don't you get to the end of the line?"

"Stay out of it, Jamie. This is between me and the little jerk here. You got that?"

"Who are you calling little?" Jake spoke up, but Tone stared down at him and grabbed his collar.

"Anthony, anything that concerns Jakey also concerns me."

"Jakey huh, that's a name. What's the matter, jerk? Need a girl to fight for you now?"

Jake went red with embarrassment and anger. All he wanted to do at that second was punch Tone as hard as he could; he knew his fist would crumple as soon as he hit Tone, but he didn't know what else to do.

Fortunately, Jamie did, and it was a good thing Jake's back was to her, so he couldn't see her narrow her eyes and give Tone the evil stare. Everyone knew about it, and everyone feared it, even Jake. When Jamie gave the stare, everyone was helpless. They had to bend to her command, even Tone.

"All right, jerk, you win this time, but next time you won't be so lucky," Tone said as he shoved Jake back, let go of his collar, and walked to the end of the line.

"See, Jamie, Tone was no problem at all."

"Yeah, you had him shaking," Jamie said halfheartedly.

"You know, you didn't have to butt in. I could have taken him myself."

"Sure, then I would have had to scrape you off the ground."

"Why didn't he bother you just then? Why did he leave you alone?"

"That's a secret. I'll tell you sometime."

"Fine, keep secrets from me. Just don't tell me anything," Jake said, trying to pretend like it hurt him.

Jamie saw right through his bad acting. "You big baby. I'll tell you some other time, OK?"

"I guess."

It was their turn to walk in. Jake followed Jamie through the long halls that made up the school. He knew them so well he could find his way with his eyes closed.

He finally reached his classroom, and his teacher was already there. She held her big, red binder book that had all her important notes. Once everyone was seated, she spoke: "Class, today I've decided to be a little out of the ordinary, and I've come up with a new seating arrangement for you."

There were some groans and some yays. Jake was a little relieved. He wouldn't have to sit by Jamie anymore. She always copied his test answers.

"Now, in the first row: Jake, Nick, Craig, Ryan, and Jamie."

Jake grabbed some of his stuff and began to move. How about that? She had placed together the only people who knew the truth about The Dangerous Four and didn't even know it.

As he moved his stuff, Craig went over to him and whispered, "She's doing something different. I wonder if she's been talking to Mrs. Maley lately."

"Who knows, but if she starts dressing weird, I'm going to start to worry."

Jake went back to his seat to grab the rest of his stuff. As he walked back to his new seat, he didn't see Tone stick his foot out until it was too late. He tripped, and papers went flying everywhere. The class erupted in laughter as Tone bent down to Jake and whispered, "I told you the next time you wouldn't be so lucky, jerk."

Jake was about ready to jump on him when Jamie stopped him. "Let it go," she whispered.

Jake scowled, but he picked up his papers and made his way to his desk. He slumped in his seat and tried to shake the whole thing off. He didn't get why Tone picked on him so much. He was a bully to everyone, but he really seemed to go for Jake. Jake honestly didn't know who was worse—while he was Jake, he had Tone to worry about, but as Left-y, there was Jeff. No matter who he was, there was always someone trying to bring him down.

After that, Jake's morning went well and lunchtime soon came. He grabbed his food and went to his usual table.

"Hey, man, sorry about what happened this morning. Tone was a real jerk. You didn't deserve that."

"Thanks, Nick, but I really don't feel like talking about it. Maybe one day he'll realize what he was doing was mean and stop. I hope it's soon," Jake said as he took a bite of his grilled chicken, "but enough about this morning. Let's get down to business."

"Yeah, like when's the next meeting going to be?"

"I'm thinking Sunday night," Jake replied.

"Are we going to be doing what I think we'll be doing?" Craig asked as his eyes widened and he smiled a bit.

"We sure are," Jake said as Jamie walked by. He called her over.

"What's up, Jakey?"

"Can you make a meeting Sunday night?"

"Sure what's going on Sunday night?"

"You'll find out then."

Jamie started to say something, but the bell rang and everyone got up to leave. As Jake walked back to class, he couldn't help but wonder where The Dangerous Four's lives were heading. Things were different now that Jamie knew their secret. What would her part be? She couldn't stay a groupie forever. Maybe she'd go with them. Maybe she'd even be one of them.

Jake shook his head at the idea. Jamie wouldn't like all the work that went into being The Dangerous Four. Plus, he doubted she could stand to be around Craig that much, but once in awhile, Jamie surprised people. Then again, maybe she just wanted to be a fan and leave the music to the real musicians. Jake decided he wouldn't worry about it now, and he hoped that the afternoon would turn out better than the morning.

CHAPTER 4

Jake's life was pretty boring for the rest of the week. He had some chores to do around the house, as well as homework. Since they didn't plan to meet for nearly a week, for a short time it seemed like The Dangerous Four were somebody else or they didn't exist at all. Of course, Jake knew better—although sometimes he wished they were somebody else. When he and the others had started the band, none of them had had any idea it was going to be so much work. Everybody enjoyed doing it, no doubt, but it was a lot for four kids.

Sometimes he wondered if, one day, it would be too much, and they'd quit. He hoped it would never come to that. He loved sneaking out at night to practice or perform. There was some danger to getting caught and people finding out, and that's why they were called The Dangerous Four.

Sunday night came, and Left-y, Rightey, and Drummey were in the clubhouse eagerly awaiting Rousey and Jamie's arrival. Drummey was looking through some sheet music while Left-y and Rightey stood in the corner reading one of the articles that had been written about them. Left-y paced back and forth for lack of anything else to do. A slight breeze blew through the door and made him shiver. Fall was coming to a close, and winter would soon be there.

Finally Left-y stopped pacing. "Where the heck is Rousey?"

"Late, as usual," Rightey said, looking up from the article. "He really should get that watch fixed."

"Yeah, but Jamie isn't here either."

Drummey looked up from his papers.

"Hey, you don't think Rousey and Jamie met up on the way here and started fighting and ..."

"Don't even finish that, Drummey," Jamie said as she stood in the doorway. Her hands were on her hips as she walked in. She had a jacket on but took it off. "For your information, I haven't seen Rousey since Friday at school, so whatever you guys were thinking, forget it."

"Calm down, Jamie. We were just wondering where Rousey is. We hadn't seen him and were wondering if you had."

"Well, I already told you, I hadn't," she said as a figure appeared in the doorway.

"Have no fear, Rousey's here!" came a loud and proud voice from the doorway. "I come giving you all the great gift of my presence."

"I think I'll return that gift," Jamie said quietly.

"You're lucky you even get to be here, you know that!"

Jamie was surprised he'd gotten so upset at her, and she was a little hurt by it. Her eyes started to water, but she quickly pushed it away. Left-y could tell she was upset.

"It's OK, Jamie. Rousey didn't mean it. You know him; he's never serious, right Rousey?"

"Uh, yeah, sure, whatever."

Jamie was still a little hurt, but she wouldn't let it bother her. She pushed it aside and then asked what she had been wondering the whole week.

"OK, guys, now that it's Sunday, you have to tell me. What is so special about Sunday night?"

"Well, if you must know, we sometimes listen to this old radio show where they play really old music, and we get ideas for our songs."

"You're kidding, right?"

"Do I look like I'm joking?"

"Just what kind of old music is playing?"

"All different types. We like a lot of the jazz and rock. That's where we get our fast-paced songs from. We get ideas from fifties songs for our voice parts. There was a lot of good singing done in that era."

"You guys are weird. Anything that old belongs on a shelf locked away in some basement or museum. There's no way anyone would listen to that stuff now."

"You didn't seem to care whenever we played a concert, did you?" Rousey asked to challenge her. "If I remember right, there were two girls who snuck backstage to get our autographs because they thought we were so great. Now, who were they again? Jamie, do you know?"

"That was Sarah's idea."

"Right, and you had nothing to do with it. And just so you get this right, we don't actually play these songs; we get ideas from them."

"Jamie, do you remember when we played you that song that didn't have an ending?"

"Yeah, I remember that."

"What'd you think of it?"

"I thought it was great. The music was a good pace, and the voices blended in harmony."

"Well, we sort of got that idea from those old songs."

"No way! I don't believe it."

"I'll prove it to you. Rousey, turn on the radio."

"With pleasure, Left-y," Rousey said as he hit the dial. It took a short time for the old radio to warm up; then they could hear static. Rousey fumbled with the dial, but when he got it, there was the same sweet style music Jamie had heard them play. This was The Dangerous Four's sound, their style.

Once the song was over, Rousey turned the volume down. "Well, what do you think?"

"I think it sounds great. I had no idea old music could sound like that. It's really cool."

"It sure is," Left-y said. "Now that everyone agrees, let's listen some more."

Everyone cheered in agreement as Rousey turned up the volume. It was a little hard to hear because of the static. Jamie thought that they should get a new radio, but Left-y said that it just wouldn't be the same. Jamie began to tap her foot to the beat as she stared out the window into the night. Man this was cool, staying out late with a bunch of friends in a secret clubhouse. Jamie really wanted to be a part of the band, but how? Maybe she could practice and, in time, join them. But first she would have to ask them—sometime tonight, but not right now, later. Right now she was enjoying the music and watching Left-y and Rousey air guitar to the song. She mainly kept her eyes on Left-y, though. He was always nice and would stick up for her when she would ask to join, but would the others let her? Jamie was beginning to get butterflies in her stomach just thinking about it, and she tried not to let it show. She focused on listening to the music for the rest of the time. When midnight came, the old DJ said that was it and left them with one final song. Once it was over, Rousey went over and shut off the radio. Everyone got up.

"Well, I guess that's it then," Rightey said, half yawning. "I'll see all of you later."

"Wait, hold up," Jamie called. "I've got to say something."

"Yeah?"

"What is it, Jamie?" Left-y asked.

Jamie looked at all of them staring at her. She knew it was now or never. She had to ask, so she cleared her throat. "Uh guys, I want all of you to know how much I enjoyed tonight. I really like the music, and I really like your music as well. I love being able to listen to you guys practice, but I want to be doing something too. So I was thinking you guys could teach me the stuff and, in time, I could join the band."

So many things happened at that moment. Jamie was relieved that she had finally asked them, Left-y just stood there staring with his mouth open, and the other three burst out laughing. Left-y started to giggle, but he stopped when he realized she was serious. He turned to the others, and then they shut up. They quickly made a huddle.

"If you guys are finished with your little laughing attack, we need to deal with this," he whispered.

"Left-y, relax," Rousey said. "She was just joking. She wouldn't ask something that stupid. How can you possibly take this seriously?"

"Because she is serious; look at her."

The four of them looked at her. She stood with her hands at her side and her jaw was moving back and fourth. Her eyes were wide.

"She does look kind of nervous," Rightey said.

"Yeah, I guess," Rousey agreed. "So, what do we tell her?"

"I've got a better idea," Drummey said. "How about we find out why she wants to join? That may give us some answers."

They talked a little more and decided that Left-y would be the one to ask Jamie everything. After all, she did have a soft spot for him. He walked up to her.

"Hey, Jamie, could we talk about this?"

"Sure, what do you want to know?"

"Well, first, why do you want to join The Dangerous Four?"

"It sounds like fun. You guys have a blast being on the stage, and I like the music."

"Lots of people like music, but they aren't in bands."

"Yeah, but some of them are. I could be one of them."

"OK, Jamie, let's just think about this for a second. How much experience have you had on the stage?"

"Do you count the time I was on the stage at school?"

"No."

"Well, in that case, none."

"And how much musical talent do you have?"

"I don't know yet."

"What do you mean, yet?"

"I've never really tried. I could be really good and not know it. And even if I'm not, I can learn if you'll teach me."

"You want me to teach you to be a rock star?"

"Not just you, Left-y, all of you. I can learn and, in time, take the stage with you. I'm already your biggest fan."

Left-y could tell he wasn't getting through. Jamie was dead set on joining them, so he decided a different approach.

"Jamie, the four of us have been together for quite awhile now. We all know how each other works, what makes us tick. Sometimes we even know what one of us will say even before he says it, and the fact is, we don't know you like that. It would take a long, long time for you to really be ready to join. Besides, I'm not sure you'd even want to be with us if you knew what it was really like."

"What do you mean? I know exactly what it's like. You guys wear masks and costumes on the stage, everyone cheers, and you guys practice here almost every night. What else do I need to know?"

"Is that all you think we do?" Left-y asked. He was a little annoyed she thought it was that easy.

"There is a lot more to us than just sneaking around and performing all the time. It's a heck of a lot of work."

"I know you guys work hard. I can work hard too."

"It's not that simple, Jamie. Since we're a well-known group now, there's a lot of pressure to always be the best. All these late-night practices can really wear someone down. Then there's the risk of someone finding out who we really are."

"Someone already did, and that worked out fine."

"And we were very lucky it did. Look, Jamie, we're thrilled that you're a fan and decided to keep our secret and all."

"Then why won't you let me join?"

"Because, we already have a full band. We have a drummer, a bass guitarist, a lead singer, and a lead guitarist, although he isn't much of one."

"Hey! I heard that!" Rousey shouted.

"I know you did. I wanted to make sure you were still there. Listen, Jamie; we've got everything we need. There's no point in adding another member. Besides, what would you do anyway?"

"I don't know. I could sing or find an instrument."

"I don't think so, Jamie. Thanks for the offer, but it just wouldn't work, OK?"

"Yeah, OK," she said sadly. She was really hurt they'd said no. She had honestly thought they'd say yes. She was getting angry, but she knew it was their choice, and she would not let it show—not in front of them, not in front of Left-y.

Things would have been fine, but then Rousey opened his mouth. "What were you thinking, Jamie? Why would we want a girl to join our band, especially you! You'd just be in the way."

That did it. Jamie was furious. Her hands clenched into fists as she stormed up to Rousey, drew her right hand back, and slapped him across the face as hard as she could. Rousey spun halfway around and fell on the floor. Then she screamed out, "I hate you all! I hope everyone finds out what jerks you really are, especially you, Rousey!"

With that, she ran out of the clubhouse. She was beginning to cry but didn't care. Left-y started after her but stopped after a couple of steps. He figured she had better be left alone. He turned back and looked at Rightey and Drummey. Their eyes were wide and their mouths open. Meanwhile, Rousey was crying out in pain:

"Ow! She slapped me. It hurts! It hurts! Someone call an ambulance; it hurts!"

Left-y stared at him on the ground while Rightey and Drummey held him down. Left-y wasn't in too big of a hurry to help him. He looked at Rousey's cheek, and sure enough, there was a nice, red handprint.

After some more whining, Rousey finally calmed down and said, "I think it went pretty well."

"You what?" Left-y asked.

"Aside from the slap and all. I told you, Left-y. That girl's crazy."

"Is that all you can say?" he asked angrily.

"Well, what else was I supposed to do? Hey, can you get me something for that slap? My cheek's beginning to sting."

"You were supposed to keep your big mouth shut. Left-y was doing a fine job without you."

"Thank you, Rightey, and no Rousey, I won't get you anything for that slap. You deserved it. Besides, that's not what I'd worry about anyway."

"And what would you worry about?"

"I'd worry about our secret."

"What are you talking about, Left-y?"

"Think about it, Rousey. The only person who knows our real identity is really mad at us right now, probably willing to do anything to get back at us. I bet there are a lot of people out there who would love to get the inside information on us, and Jamie could do it. You see what I'm saying?"

"Do you really think Jamie would do that?" Drummey asked.

"I don't know. She's really mad, but Jamie's got a lot of common sense. She loves The Dangerous Four too much to ruin it, or does she?"

"If she tells people about us," Rightey started, "that would mean the end of it for us. There would be no more sneaking around. We'd be done."

"My dad would find out," Left-y said. "He'd ground me till I was thirty."

"Man, that's terrible to think about now. Maybe we should have let her in the band."

"What?" the three of them gasped at Drummey's idea.

"Well, if Jamie was in the band, then we wouldn't have to worry about her telling anyone because she would be exposed too."

"I get it!" Left-y said loudly. "It'd be like insurance. That's why none of us worry about any of us running off and telling anyone—because then they'd be exposed too."

"Hey, Left-y, can we let him go yet?" Rightey asked.

"Yeah, I'm sorry, Left-y," Rousey said sincerely. "I've calmed down now."

"Let him go," Left-y said, as Rightey and Drummey got off of Rousey. Rousey got up and shook out his arms and legs. He cracked his neck to one side and then the other.

"Thank you," he said, and then he made a run for Left-y, but Rightey and Drummey stopped him.

"Take it easy, Rousey. Left-y didn't do anything."

"Didn't do anything? Are you two blind? He's the whole reason we're in this mess. I warned you, Left-y. Girls are trouble, but you wouldn't listen. You had to bring your stupid girlfriend here. Now she knows everything, and she's going to ruin it for all of us! You think I did this? None of this would have happened if you would have just listened to me; but no—you had to have your way!"

Rightey and Drummey let go of him. He walked out, and as he passed Left-y, he spoke in a whisper so only Left-y could hear him: "I hope you're happy, and I hope you know what you're doing because, if your girlfriend breaks us up, it's your fault."

"She's not me girlfriend; we're only friends, Rousey. Hey, Rousey …"

"Let him go, Left-y. He needs to be alone."

Left-y walked over to the table and sat down on the stool. "What a mess."

"Don't take it personally, Left-y. Rousey's been through a lot lately, especially at home."

Drummey was right. Rousey's parents had been fighting a lot. They yelled at each other almost every night. The topic didn't seem to matter. They fought about everything. Rousey pretended it didn't bother him. He laughed and smiled all the time at school and worked really hard on the late-night practices, but everyone could tell it was getting to him. He couldn't talk to his parents about it. Left-y and the others did their best, but there is only so much that friends can do. It was hard to see Rousey like this. He and Left-y had been friends for so long. Rousey was always high-strung, and Left-y knew it would someday get him into trouble. Now it had, and not only Rousey, but all of The Dangerous Four were in danger of being exposed. They had all faced challenges together before and won. He just hoped they would be able to win this one too.

CHAPTER 5

Jamie ran as fast as she could through the field, the whole time trying to hold back her tears. She didn't really care which way she ran or where she was going, just that it was as far away from that clubhouse as possible. After a few minutes of running full blast, she tripped over a rock and fell face-first into some soft mud. She couldn't control herself any more. She just lay there and cried.

It hurt so much inside. She was sad, angry, embarrassed, and hurt all at the same time. Why did she do that? Rousey was right. What *had* she been thinking? She began to sob again. After a bit, she pulled herself together enough to look around, only to realize she was lost, and she began to cry all over again.

After a little bit, she ran out of tears and just listened to the cold night. There were a couple of faint bird calls here and there but nothing else. It was very quiet. She hoped no one had heard her.

Jamie actually felt a little embarrassed about crying like that, but she was so upset. She figured it was pretty dumb of her to think they would have just let her in like that. Now everything was going to be weird between them.

By "them" of course she meant herself and Jake, or Left-y. It didn't matter what she called him. She had opened herself up to him, and he had rejected her. But it was just her talent, or lack thereof, not her. Maybe there was still hope. If there was, it would be a long time before she told him the truth. What in the world was she going to do now? Then she had an idea. She would show those boys. She'd get an instrument and learn to play on her own. She'd get good, really good, so good they'd beg her to join.

With that, she made a fist and smacked the ground, but she forgot she was in mud and it splattered up in her face.

She stood up and looked around. After a short while, she realized that she had run off at an angle and was south of her house. She had to squint, but she could just barely see her block. Jamie began to walk toward it. Her pace quickened into a sprint, then a full-out run. She ran and ran. All the while thinking about what she was going to do. Her sadness was fading, and her determination was growing. What instrument would she play? What could they use that she had? Of course! She had the perfect idea. Hopefully her dad hadn't gotten rid of it.

She reached the edge of the field that met the end of her backyard and stopped to catch her breath. She then climbed into her room and shut her window. She changed clothes and went into the bathroom to clean up. She turned on the light and looked at herself in the mirror. Her face was covered in mud. She ran the water and washed it off. As she cleaned up, she looked at herself in the mirror and made a promise.

"I will learn to play, and I will get my dream, and nothing, nothing is going to stand in my way!"

She then put her hands over her mouth. Had she said that out loud? Had anyone heard her?

Jamie got the answer. She heard heavy footsteps coming down the hall. She knew they were her dad's.

"Jamie, what are you doing in there?"

"Uh, nothing, Dad, just going getting a drink."

"Well, hurry up. It's the middle of the night. Go back to bed."

As he left, Jamie put her ear to the door and she heard him mumble, "Lazy, good-for-nothing kid, wakes me up in the middle of the night for no reason ..."

Jamie felt her heart sink a bit. Why did he always say things like that? She knew deep down he loved her, but still, why did he have to say mean things?

Jamie finished cleaning up and went back to her bedroom. She got into bed and tried to relax. The more she thought about her decision, the better she felt. She would check it out when her parents weren't around and wouldn't ask questions. She was happy with her plan, and after a short while, she fell asleep.

The next few days at school were rough on Jake. He would try to talk to Jamie or even get her attention, but every time he tried, she just walked by like he wasn't even there, and it was beginning to get to him.

"I don't get it," he said Wednesday at the lunch table. "She won't even look at me. I can't believe I'm going to say this, but I think I'm beginning to miss her and all the little things she does."

"Like calling you Jakey all the time?" Ryan asked.

"Even that," Jake replied. "I just wish things were back to normal."

"That will take some time," Nick said. "I think we really hurt her."

"So do I, but she's not the only one hurting," Jake said as Craig sat down and began to eat. The two of them hadn't really made up either. They talked to each other, but he could tell Craig was still mad.

"Hey, Craig, how you doing?"

"Fine," Craig replied without looking up.

"So uh, some math assignment, huh?"

"Huh," Craig replied, again without looking up.

Jake gave up trying to talk to Craig and drowned his thoughts in his sandwich, his peanut butter and strawberry sandwich. Normally he hated combos like that, but today it tasted really good.

He saw Jamie walk by and raised his hand to call her over, but she looked past him and just kept on walking to the table with Sarah and a bunch of girls.

"I see what you mean," Ryan said. "She completely ignored you."

"I know. She's been like this all week. I just wish she would talk to me."

"Why, so you can tell her more stuff?" Craig said rudely.

"Hey, he said a full sentence."

"Shut up, Nick. I'm not in the mood to be funny."

"Craig, please. You've got to let this go," Jake pleaded. "I can't stand this any more. What's it going to take to forgive me, huh? What's it going to take?"

"You want to know what it's going to take?" Just then the bell rang. Craig got up and leaned over the table to Jake and said, "Get things back to the way they were, before all this happened."

"You know that's something I can't do."

"Then it's going to be a long time before we're friends again," he said as he walked off.

Ryan went over to Jake. "Don't take it so hard, Jake. I know Craig, and I say you two will be friends again before the end of the week."

"I hope you're right," Jake said as he got up and started off to class. Jake was too caught up in everything, so he didn't watch where he was going and bumped right into Tone.

"Well, if it isn't the little jerk. Where are you going?" Tone asked as he got in Jake's way and pushed him back but held onto his shirt.

"I'm going back to class, where you should be. Oh wait; do you have detention or something?"

"You've got a real big mouth, jerk. You know that? And I think it's time I shut it up, with my fist."

"Uh, no thanks, I already ate lunch," Jake said, getting more and more nervous.

"This is it, jerk. This time your little girlfriend isn't here to save you," Tone said, as he pulled his right hand back and prepared to smack Jake a big one.

Jake shut his eyes and waited for the pain, but it didn't come. He opened his eyes and looked around to find a teacher standing right behind Tone. His hand was around Tone's fist, stopping the punch.

"Looks like you and I should have a nice, long talk in detention, young man," the teacher said as he led Tone down the hall. Tone had a disgusted look on his face, but there was nothing he could do.

Jake had never been so happy to see a teacher. He figured Tone would try again, but that could be dealt with later. Right now he had to get back to class.

He made it just before the bell rang. As he sat down and began to work, he noticed that his usual teacher was gone, and Mrs. Maley was watching the class. Even though she dressed crazy and was a little strange, he liked her. She was a pretty slack teacher. Every now and again, Jake would try to look back and steal a glance at Jamie, but Craig always blocked his view and made a face. After a few times, he figured it was hopeless. He really missed Craig and Jamie as well, but it was different with Jamie. He wasn't sure who he missed more. He'd almost say Jamie, but that was too weird. All of this was just too weird.

He started to erase a line and dropped his pencil in the process. It fell onto the floor and began to roll back. Jake got out of his seat to go after it. The pencil had rolled past Nick's desk and stopped right at Craig's. Jake reached for it, but Craig put his foot on it. Jake tried to get it, but Craig wouldn't let up.

Finally, Jake whispered to Craig, "Give me my pencil back, Craig."

"Well, let me think about that. No."

"I mean it. Give it back."

"Why should I?"

"Boys, is there a problem?"

"Uh, no, Mrs. Maley. No problem at all," Jake replied. Then he whispered, "Except Craig won't stop being a baby and give me back my pencil. I mean it, Craig, now!"

"You want it?'

"Yeah!"

"All right, here it comes," Craig said as he quickly punched Jake in the stomach.

Jake took a step back to catch his breath. He was not ready for that at all, but if it was a fight Craig wanted, then it was a fight he was going to get. Jake shoved him back hard—so hard Craig fell right out of his seat and smacked his head against a neighboring desk. Craig sat there for a second, shook his head, stood up, jumped onto his desk, and took a leap at Jake. He landed right on him, and the two of them fell down and began punching each other.

"Fight! Fight! Fight!" a kid screamed.

"Boys! Boys! That's enough! Stop this at once!" Mrs. Maley screamed as she ran over to them and grabbed each one by the shirt.

"You boys can spend the rest of the week in detention for the way you've behaved. Let's see what the principal has to say about this, shall we?"

Jake and Craig both sat in the front office waiting for the principal. Neither of them looked at each other or said a word. Finally, the door opened and a hand motioned for them to come in. They both went in and sat down in chairs in front of the principal's desk.

"Jake and Craig, I am disappointed to hear that you two were fighting in class," the principal said as he glared at them through his small, round glasses. He was a middle-aged, heavier man, but he didn't let that slow him down. He knew kids, and he knew them well. "Well, boys, why don't you tell me what happened?"

"It's his fault," both of them said at the same time.

"I will listen to both sides. How did this whole fight start?"

"Well see," Jake started, "I dropped my pencil and went to get it, but Craig wouldn't let me."

"Craig, is this true?"

"Not even close. He threw it at me, and it hit me right in the eye, see."

"I did not, you liar! He's lying!"

"I am not; you're the liar!" Craig shouted as he punched Jake again.

But this time Jake was ready for it. He blocked the punch and started after Craig.

"Boys! Enough!" the principal shouted.

Jake and Craig stopped at once and stared at him. He was standing up, arms fully stretched out and fists on top of his desk as he leaned toward them. His eyebrows were bent down as he glared at them hard. He may have been middle-aged, but he sure hid it well. His voice was hard and stern. This guy would even make Tone uneasy. After a few seconds of just staring at each other, Jake and Craig sat down, and so did the principal. He finally made his decision.

"I think the best thing for the two of you is some quiet time after school. The two of you will have detention one hour after school for the rest of the week."

"But that's …" Craig started, but one stern look from the principal, and he changed his mind.

"Exactly what I think we need," he finished.

"Now that we have that straightened out, you two can go on back to class. I'll call your parents and let them know to pick you up a little later. Report to the detention room number 104 after school."

Jake and Craig both left and walked back to class in silence. Jake felt horrible. He had never had detention before in his life, and now he did, and his parents were going to know. What would they say? Even worse, he was in it with Craig, and right now he hated Craig. Craig probably thought that it was Jake's fault he got detention too. It probably wasn't as big of deal for him. Craig had had detention before, but this time he had someone to blame it on.

Once back in class, Jake spent the rest of the afternoon trying to look back at Jamie, but he just kept on seeing Craig. This was the worst fight the two of them had ever had. He hoped they would get through this, or it could be the end of The Dangerous Four. No, they had to get through this. They just had to.

Jamie noticed Jake trying to look at her as she read her book. Jake had been doing that all day, but Craig always got in the way before they could make eye contact. Why did Craig keep getting in the middle? Was Jake trying to apologize? As much as Jamie wanted it, she doubted it. She had seen the fight and figured Jake and Craig were having a disagreement over something. What was it? Could it be her? Could Jake want her in the band and Craig didn't? As much as Jamie wanted to believe that, she doubted that as well.

Jamie glanced at the clock and went back to reading her book. It was almost time to go. She couldn't wait to get home and get to practicing. The sooner she could play, the better. She could talk to Jake again. She really missed him.

The bell rang and school was over, or at least it was over for everyone else. Jake still had an hour to go—in detention. He got his books and slowly walked down the hall to room 104. He had never been there before, so he hoped they would let him do some homework or read a book or something.

As he neared the door, he began to wonder if it would really be so bad. Maybe there would be other kids, and they could all play games. It could actually be fun.

He reached the room, opened the door, and walked in. It was nothing like he expected. There was a teacher he didn't recognize and only one other person, Tone. He looked up and gave Jake an evil grin. Jake wondered if things could get any worse, and he got his answer. As soon as he sat down, Craig burst into the room.

"I'll have my usual chair, teach," he said casually.

"Just take a seat and keep quiet. There is no talking of any kind. At the end of the hour, you can talk all you want."

Jake sat in his chair. To his left, Craig sat chewing on a pencil. To his right, Tone sat building up a supply of spit wads. Jake knew they were all for him. He had to get out of there. The hour would be up soon. He checked the clock. Only five minutes had passed. He laid his head down. Maybe he could just sleep the hour away.

"Get your head up, young man!"

So much for that. He was going to go crazy if something didn't happen fast. It was just his luck that something did. There was a loud thud that made everyone jerk their heads to the window. A playground ball had hit the window quite hard. The teacher rushed over and saw a group of kids running from the window.

"Get back here!" the teacher yelled. Then he turned to Jake and the others. "I'm going to be right back, so don't try anything."

He rushed out of the room, leaving Jake alone with Tone. Tone's evil smile grew even bigger than before, and he cracked his knuckles.

"Looks like your luck has finally run out," Tone said as he got up and started toward Jake.

"Tone, think about this. Aren't you in enough trouble?"

"Maybe, but this is going to make it all worth it. Who's going to save you now, jerk? There's no girl here to fight for you, no teacher to protect you, and Craig isn't about to help you either. You're all alone. Oh yes, it's all worth it."

He made a couple of more advances toward Jake, and Jake got out of his seat.

"All right then" he said, his hands clenched in fists, to try to hide the shaking. "You want me, here I am!"

Tone drew back his fist and began to throw a punch.

"Aaahhh!" came a scream from behind Jake as Craig leaped out of his seat, jumped up on Jake's, and jumped straight into Tone. Tone was so surprised that he almost lost his balance. Jake saw his chance and took it. He drew back his fist and punched Tone in the gut as hard as he could. Tone bent over from the plow, forgetting that Craig was still on him. The weight was so much that Tone lost his balance and fell over as Craig pounded on his back and head. Jake got in a couple of more shots before they heard the footsteps of the teacher coming back. They both rushed to their seat and acted busy. The teacher came in and looked at Tone on the floor.

"What happened in here?"

"Th ... those two," Tone choked out, "they jumped me and hit me."

"Us?" Jake and Craig said in unison. Then Craig added, "We were just sitting here, and Tone started showing off by standing on his desk. He fell just before you came in."

"Tone, I think we need to have a little talk. Why don't you spend the rest of your detentions in the other room. Let's go."

The teacher led Tone out, leaving Jake and Craig together. Jake looked over at Craig and said, "Thanks, man. You saved me there."

"Don't worry about it, Jake. If anyone's going to be beating you up, it's going to be me, and maybe Jamie."

"That's not funny."

"Yeah, it is. Besides, it is kind of my fault you're here."

"Craig, are you apologizing?"

"Sort of."

"Well, I'm sorry too. I agree with you. I wish things could go back to the way they were too, but there's nothing any of us can do."

"So, what do we do now?"

"We make the most of it. We have to get to Jamie somehow. Maybe she could do something with the band without actually performing; I don't know."

"Do you think she'll tell anyone our secret?"

"I doubt it. If she hasn't told anyone by now, I doubt she ever will."

"Jake, you know I don't like Jamie being near or having anything to do with the band, but I finally think you're right. She somehow has to say connected with us. Anything's better than this, but how do we do it?"

"I have no idea, but we've got the rest of this hour, not to mention an hour tomorrow and an hour Friday to think about it, and with the two of us going at it, we just might come up with something."

CHAPTER 6

Jake's week ended a lot better than it had begun. He and Craig were friends again and were putting their heads together trying to come up with what to do about Jamie. Jake had to face his parents and explain to them about getting detention. They heard him out and decided to ground him for the rest of the week. Jake was relieved they didn't go further. He'd spent the days with the others trying to figure out the whole Jamie thing, and they'd decided that The Dangerous Four ought to have a meeting Sunday night to figure out what to do.

Left-y, Rightey, and Drummey were all waiting in the clubhouse for Rousey to show up.

"I can't believe he's late again," Left-y said as he paced up and down the clubhouse. It was eleven thirty-five, and still no sign of Rousey. "Where could he be? He knows we have a meeting."

"Sometimes I wonder if he does this on purpose."

"No I don't, Drummey," Rousey said as he burst through the door. He was panting loudly, and the right side of his face was all scratched up.

"What happened?" Rightey asked. "You look like you hit the dirt."

"I did. I was riding really fast on the last street just before the field starts. I guess I hit a patch of ice and slid. I fell on my side, but don't worry, my guitar hand's OK."

"Yeah, that's what we were worried about. How could you slide on ice? It's too warm for that."

"I guess it isn't, Left-y. It is almost Thanksgiving. Wait a minute. What are you doing here? Aren't you grounded?"

"Only for the weekend."

"It's twenty to midnight. Wouldn't your parents be a little upset if they found out you went off being grounded a little early?"

"Probably, but they don't have to know. Besides, they grounded Jake. They didn't say a thing about Left-y."

"Good point," Rousey said as he walked farther into the club-house and rubbed his hands together. "Shall we get started? It's Sunday night, so let's hear some music."

"Not yet, Rousey," Drummey said holding up his hand. "We've got some business first."

"OK, what is it?"

"We've got to figure out what to do about Jamie."

"Oh yeah. What do we have so far?"

"Not much, just that Left-y should be the one to talk to her."

"Of course it should be him. Jamie's in love with him."

"Oh, not this again!" Rightey said as he put his hands over his ears and began to hum.

"That doesn't matter," Drummey said as Rightey stopped humming. "You two get along the best. If she'll listen to anyone, she'll listen to Left-y."

"But what do I say?"

"I don't know. Just tell her we've thought about it, and we would like to give her a chance at doing something with the band or something like that."

"That sounds easy enough," Left-y said as he paced from one side to the other. He thought it over and liked it.

Rousey interrupted his thoughts. "But wait, what if she gets mad at us, or she says she doesn't want to be with us anymore?"

"That's her decision," Left-y answered, as he turned around and faced the three of them. "At least we did our part, and if she doesn't want that, fine. Things go back to the way they were."

He hung onto those words for a few seconds. A very small part of him was hoping that she would say no. Then everything would go back to the way it was before all this happened. It would just be the four of them. Left-y hated himself for thinking that. He couldn't hide it any longer—he did like her, but she made things a lot harder. Somehow though, it all seemed worth it. She'd say yes. She had to. He shook his head as if coming out of a dream and found everyone staring at him.

"So, you guys OK with the plan?"

They all nodded.

"All right then. Business is over. Let's listen to some tunes!"

Jake got a few comments about the fight Monday at school, but those quickly died away. Thinking back, the whole thing seemed rather silly; even Craig agreed that it was dumb.

"Yeah, it was pretty stupid of us," Jake said between mouthfuls. "I say we promise never to fight again."

"That'll last a week," Ryan said. Nick laughed a bit.

Jake barely heard him. His thoughts were elsewhere. Jamie was sitting with Sarah and a bunch of girls a few tables over. She got up to throw away her lunch, and Jake watched every move out of the corner of his eye. Jamie didn't so much as even look toward him. He watched her sit back down and sighed.

"You've got to do it, man," Ryan said as he took a sip of milk.

"Yeah, do it now," Nick urged.

He looked at Craig, and Craig nodded. "Now," he mouthed.

"All right, here it goes," he muttered as he got up and dumped his trash. He then walked over to Jamie's table. Jamie noticed him but ignored him.

"Uh, Jamie, could I talk to you for a ..."

The bell rang, and she got up.

"Humh," she said as she got up and turned away.

"Ooo, shot down!" Sarah said and giggled.

Jake rolled his eyes and went after her. He half walked, half ran trying to keep up. They were almost to the classroom when he got to her. He ran in front of her to block the way.

"Jamie," he said firmly, but kindly, "we need to talk, and we need to talk now."

Jamie crossed her arms in front of her and had a sour expression on her face. Jake could tell she was not happy to see him.

"What do you want?" she asked flatly.

"I want to talk about that night."

"What night?" her expression did not change.

"You know what night, Jamie. The night you were, well, you know where."

"Look, Jake, I get it. You guys don't need me, nor do you want me. What else is there to talk about?"

"That's just it. Look, your uh, idea, was so unexpected, we didn't know what to say. We all got a little upset, and things got out of hand."

"They sure did," Jamie said as she uncrossed her arms. She seemed to be listening more. Jake hoped so.

"Anyway, we talked it over some more, and we think you could really help us."

"Help you how?"

"We didn't realize how much it meant to you, and if you want, we could work with you and, in time, you could even play with us," Jake said smoothly. He was quite pleased with himself.

Jamie seemed to be softening. She walked over to him and said, "So you mean I'd get to play with you? So, am I supposed to be honored or something?" Jamie didn't know why she was saying it. Her mind and heart were jumping for joy that Jake had said this, but her anger was beginning to take over.

Jake was a little taken aback by what she had said. "Uh, I guess if you feel that way, that's great," Jake didn't know what else to say. He could tell she was getting upset.

Then she let him have it. She walked up to him and said very quietly, "Do you have any idea what you four put me through? You guys really hurt me, and I'm supposed to forget it all just like that? I don't think so!"

"So you're not interested?"

"I never said that," she snapped. "When would this be?"

"Our next meeting is Sunday."

"Well, I don't know if I'll come."

"Fine," Jake said as he clenched his fists. He couldn't believe Jamie was acting like this, and after all the work he'd gone through to get the others to let him do this. "The meeting's next Sunday, with or without you. I hope you really think about it because it's going to be a long, long time before *you* get an invitation like this again." With that Jake walked away from her and into class.

Jamie was stunned. How in the world could she have said that, and to Jake too? He had stood up for her when no one else would, and she had been so mean to him. She was angry with the guys for laughing at her, but now they wanted her in. They wanted her to be part of the coolest band ever, and she had destroyed her only chance, or had she? Hadn't Jake said there was another meeting? Yes! But when was it? It was on the weekend. Saturday? No Sunday. Of course! Sunday night. That was almost a week away. Could she wait that long? She'd have to, but would it even be worth it? What if they just laughed at her when she tried to play? She didn't have much of an ear for music, but she could play a few notes. Maybe that would be enough. There was only one way to know for sure. She'd go. That much was for sure, and if they laughed at her again, she'd have her answer once and for all.

CHAPTER 7

Jake didn't talk to Jamie for the rest of the week, not after what had happened. The weekend came, but everyone was waiting for Sunday night. It came as it usually did, right after Sunday afternoon and before Monday morning.

Jamie had never been so eager to get to bed. When the coast was clear, she got up, got dressed, grabbed her instrument, and quietly opened her window. An ice-cold wind rushed into her room. Jamie shivered. She had forgotten it was the end of November as she grabbed her jacket and began to make her way toward the clubhouse.

"Do you think she'll come?" Left-y asked to anyone who would listen.

"Hard to say," Rightey replied. "Either she will, or she won't."

"You're a lot of help. What do you think, Drummey?"

"I think Rousey should get a new watch. He's late again."

"I mean about Jamie."

"Oh, I don't know. Why don't you ask her?"

Drummey pointed past Left-y, and he turned his head to see Jamie walk in. She looked extremely nervous, possibly worried. In her right hand, she held a strange-looking black case. Left-y guessed it was her instrument, but he had no idea what it was. It was too small for a guitar and the wrong shape. He swallowed and choked out a, "Hi."

"Hi," she replied quietly as she walked across the room and stood against the wall.

"Do you want to sit down?" Rightey asked.

"No thanks," she said quickly.

"What's in the case?" Drummey asked.

"You'll find out," she said just as quickly. "Can we do this now?"

"Not without Rousey."

"Do we really have to wait for him, Left-y?" Jamie said through gritted teeth.

Left-y nodded. Now she was calling him by his stage name. At least she was talking to him again. He was making progress. "Yes, we have to wait for him. He's part of the band, and he's our friend. He'd wait for us."

"Sure he would," Jamie replied with a little sarcasm. "I hope he gets here soon."

"Like, how about now?" Left-y said, as Rousey walked through the door.

"Sorry I'm late, but my watch stopped again. Maybe I should get a new one."

"We've only been saying that every meeting," Drummey said with a smile.

"Let's just get started," Jamie urged.

"Boy, someone's in a hurry," Rousey shot to her.

"I just want to get this over with. You can laugh at me then."

"I may just do that."

"Hold it!" Left-y yelled, as he got between them and pushed them both back.

"No one is going to laugh at anybody," he said glaring at Rousey. "Got it?"

"Got it," Rousey said as he went to a corner. The four of them got their instruments and set up. Jamie was amazed how fast they were. The four of them really knew what they were doing.

Once they were set up, all of them looked at her and waited. Jamie opened her case and pulled out an old, dirty saxophone.

"A sax," Left-y said surprised.

"You mean an old sax," Rightey corrected.

"No, you mean an old, dirty sax," Rousey added and smiled.

"OK, we all know what it is, but can you play it?"

"Can I play it? Just you watch, or should I say, listen," she said, as she slowly raised the sax to her lips. All of them waited to hear. She had never been so nervous. Her hands quivered as she placed them in the correct spot.

"Brace yourself," Rousey whispered to everyone.

Jamie blew into her sax and it squeaked. All four of them flinched.

"Wait! That doesn't count!" she said quickly.

"All right, Jamie," Left-y said. "Just take your time."

Jamie realized she was really hot, so she took off her jacket and threw her shoulders back a bit. She put the sax back to her lips and, with a newfound confidence, she blew into it, and out came the sweetest note any of them had ever heard. Then she made another note, the next one up the scale, then another, and another, and another until she got all the way up and down the scale. She even added a few to make it sound fancier.

When she had finished, she looked at the four of them to realize their mouths were hanging wide open, and their eyes were the biggest she'd ever seen. They were all speechless. Jamie didn't know if this was a good thing or a bad thing.

Left-y finally broke the silence: "How long have you been at this?"

"Since the last time I was here."

"Professional lessons?"

"No, just on my own."

"Jamie, you were here like two weeks ago. You mean to tell me you learned to do that in two weeks?"

"About that, yeah."

The four of them looked at each other and nodded.

Drummey spoke: "Well, if you can learn that on your own, just imagine what you can learn by practicing with us."

Jamie's heart skipped a beat.

"You mean, I'm in? I'm one of you guys now?"

"Not quite yet," Left-y said. "There's a lot you need to learn first; consider yourself in training. You're good, Jamie, real good. Maybe a little rough, but you play like one of us. If you practice with us, I'd say you'll be ready for the stage by summer."

"Great!" Jamie exclaimed as she threw her arms around Left-y. She was so excited, she almost knocked him over.

"Ugh, you're welcome, Jamie. You can let go now," Left-y choked out.

She finally let go of Left-y, and he smiled and turned to the others.

"We've got a bit of time left. Why don't we listen to some tunes on a Sunday night."

Rousey turned on the radio and they all listened to the jamming tunes. There was a great drum solo in one of the songs and Left-y saw Drummey jot down a few notes on some sheet music. No doubt he was getting an idea for a new song. After a while, the DJ said it was time to go and ended the show. Left-y turned off the radio and checked his watch.

"Whoa, it's after midnight; party's over."

Even though he'd said it, he really didn't want to go. None of them did, but they did have school the next day, and their parents would wonder why they were all so tired, so the five of them picked everything up and headed for home.

◆　　◆　　◆

Jamie was walking on air all the way back. She couldn't believe they'd said yes. She was in! She was now part of The Dangerous Four. The only thing she didn't like was she couldn't tell anyone about it, not even Sarah, and Sarah was her best friend.

As Jamie walked through the field, she thought about the upcoming week. Thursday was Thanksgiving, and she had a lot to be thankful for. She and Jake had made up and were talking again. Even Rousey had something nice to say about her. Everything was going great.

She reached her backyard and looked up. There were big, heavy clouds in the night sky. She also noticed something falling from them. Rain? No, too slow. She held out her arm and discovered it was snow—the first snowfall of the year. Maybe school would be canceled, but she doubted it as she climbed up the little shed and into her room. She got into bed and tried to sleep, but her mind was racing. What exciting adventures lay ahead for her with The Dangerous Four? For her and Jake, or Left-y for that matter? And why was Rousey always so mean to her? What had she ever done to him? Was he afraid of her? But why? Boys sure were strange she decided, as she turned over and fell asleep.

CHAPTER 8

Jake woke up and got ready for school in the usual way, except a little slowly, and just barely missed the bus, so his mom had to give him a ride. She was a little upset that he'd been late again but took him nonetheless. Once at school, he looked around for his friends and found them over at the tetherball. It had snowed the night before, just enough to cover the ground, so the kids had to drag their shoes to uncover the boundary lines. Inside the circle, the snow had either been removed or packed down from everyone stepping on it. Jake slid up to the end of the line, just as Jamie had gotten out. She joined him.

"So, how was your weekend?" he asked innocently, as if he didn't know.

"Oh, pretty dull, nothing out of the ordinary," Jamie replied just as innocently. Then she smiled at him.

He smiled back at their little secret. The bell rang a few seconds later, and everybody rushed to the line. The rest of the morning was boring—until lunchtime.

Jamie tried to catch up with Jake, but he was too fast. By the time she got to the cafeteria, Jake was already in line with people behind him. Jamie figured he must be really hungry as she felt something tug on her shirt. She turned around, and it was Sarah.

"Hi," Jamie said.

"Hey, where have you been? I haven't seen you in like, forever."

"Sarah, we talked over the weekend."

"Yeah, but that's not the same. We haven't seen each other or done anything since last week. We should figure out what we're going to do over the long weekend while we eat. I'll save you a spot."

"Thanks Sarah, except ..."

"Except what?"

"Except I was going to sit with Jake today."

"Oh, why? You never sat with him before?"

"Well, we're friends again; plus, I told him I would."

"And you didn't think to tell me? Well, I guess I'll see you later."

"Sarah, I didn't mean it like that," Jamie said quickly. She could tell Sarah was hurt.

"No, that's OK," Sarah said "Sit with whoever you want."

Jamie sighed as she got in line. She felt bad about not sitting with Sarah, but this was business.

"So, when's the next meeting?" Craig asked, as Jamie sat down.

"Saturday night. Nick's going out of town for Thanksgiving, but he'll be back by then. Everyone OK with that?"

Everyone nodded.

"Good." Then he looked at Jamie and smiled. "This will be your fist meeting. I hope you're ready."

"Oh, I'm ready all right."

"Good. Enough for now. Let's eat."

Jamie didn't know why the week seemed to drag on since it was so short, but finally Wednesday evening came, and school was over. She lay on her bed reading a magazine when the phone rang.

"Hello," she said into the phone.

"Hey, Jamie, it's Sarah. What's up?"

"Nothing much; reading a magazine. What are you up to?"

"Watching some TV. Hey, I called some of our friends, and they went to have a sleepover. You up for it?"

"Yes, definitely."

"Great! It's going to be at my place, and guess what."

"What?"

"Kayla told me she could get a great movie, and," Jamie could tell Sarah was really excited about it as she whispered into the phone, "it's rated PG-13."

"No!"

"Yes! It's going to be great!"

"I'll say, so when is it?"

"It's Saturday night."

Jamie's heart sank. Her first practice was Saturday night. What was she going to do?

"Uh, Sarah, I just remembered. I have something going on Saturday night. Can you make it any other night?"

"No, I can't. What's going on Saturday night?"

"I'm doing stuff."

"With who?"

"People."

"Which people, boys or girls?"

"What difference does that make? Look, if you really want to know, I'm doing something with Jake," Jamie said into the phone. It wasn't like she was lying; she really was doing something with Jake. It just happened to include a few other people.

"OK, Jamie, that's fine," Sarah said without much effort.

"Sarah, it's not that I don't want to go. I do, I really do."

"I'm sure you do. I get it. You're busy. Maybe we'll do it some other time."

"Yes, for sure. Call me."

"Sure, Jamie, see you later. Bye," Jamie heard Sarah say as she put down the phone.

She knew Sarah was upset, but what else was she supposed to do? She was with the band now. She had other commitments. She wanted to tell Sarah this more than anything. The two of them shared all sorts of secrets. Sarah was the only one Jamie had trusted with how she felt about Jake. She hoped that this wouldn't ruin their friendship. She liked Jake, and she loved the fact she was in The Dangerous Four, but she wanted Sarah as her friend. Their friendship would last. It had to. Besides, it's not like she was going to have practices every night.

That made her remember her first practice was only a few days away. She imagined what it would be like—all five of them jamming to the fast-paced beat of their newest hit song. She could almost hear it now. Jamie didn't know it, but she began to tap her foot to the imaginary beat. She couldn't wait until then. It was going to rock!

◆   ◆   ◆

Jamie counted down the days until Saturday night came. Once she got to the clubhouse, she found Left-y, Rightey, and Drummey already there.

"Man, and I thought I was going to be early."

Drummey checked his watch.

"You are early. It's eleven twenty-five. If only Rousey could do that."

Jamie smiled and walked in. Left-y and Rightey laughed, but they were cut short.

"I didn't think that was very funny," Rousey said as he came in. "I finally got my watch fixed, and I'm early this time."

"Actually, you're not. It's eleven thirty-one. Check and see."

"That's not fair! I was so close!"

"Oh who cares what time it is?" Rightey yelled with his hands in the air. "Let's just start the practice."

"Great idea," Left-y said as he looked over at Jamie.

"Well, Jamie, if you're going to be in our band, then you'll have to learn our songs. The four of us have been putting our heads together trying to come up with a way to put your sax into the songs. We're going for more of a jazz style now. We think it will work real well, but first you have to learn to play a little better. We'll start with a real easy song."

Left-y picked up some sheet music from the table. He handed the pages out to everyone as they got their instruments ready. They had decided to hold off on their songs for a few more practices. The five of them worked on the simple nursery rhyme, each one of them doing his or her part and the boys doing their best to help Jamie. She struggled at first, but after awhile, she got the hang of it. Everyone encouraged her. Even Rousey said she wasn't terrible. By the end of the night, they all had the rhyme down cold.

"This is great!" Jamie said, as she put her sax down. "So, when am I going to learn your songs? And when am I going to be ready for the stage?"

"Whoa, slow down, Jamie. Just take it one practice at a time. You're good, but you've got a lot to learn before you hit the stage."

"You really think I'm good?" she asked sweetly.

Left-y looked directly into her eyes and whispered, "I thought you were great."

Jamie's mouth went dry. She tried to swallow but couldn't. She finally managed to choke out a thank you.

Left-y nodded and turned away to start picking up. Jamie knew for sure now. She liked him, and he had to like her. She would tell him, but when, and how? It had to be when they were together, but just them, no one else around. The next meeting? No, the others would be around too. It would have to be some other time.

"Someday," she said almost silently.

Jamie and The Dangerous Four spent the month of December teaching her the basics of performing. There was a lot more to being a performer on the stage than just playing music. The Dangerous Four had a certain style that she hadn't noticed before. She had to learn how to walk and pose when on stage and also how to hold her sax while playing. She found that everyone moved a certain way while playing. Since they held their own instruments, they couldn't really dance to the music, but they didn't stand still and just play them either. It took her a while to finally be comfortable moving around while playing at the same time. Left-y, Rightey, Rousey, and Drummey spent time rewriting their songs to accommodate her part. Jamie did all she could to learn and work like one of The Dangerous

Four, and they did their part to help her. Even Rousey gave her some pointers on how to move to the beat with style.

"There you go, Jamie. That looks awesome," Left-y said once they finished a song. The last few notes trailed off into the night, leaving them in silence.

"Thanks, Left-y; I didn't realize there was so much to all of this."

"And we're not even close to being done," Drummey said as he held up some more sheet music. "We're only about halfway through our songs."

"Oh!" Jamie gasped, as she put her hand to her head and fell against the wall. "I've been working on this for a month now, and we're only halfway through?"

"About that, yeah."

"Oh, man! When is this going to end? I want to go on stage!"

"We know you do, Jamie," Left-y said, trying to sympathize with her. "We just want you to be ready; that's all. Besides, we've already started promoting you."

Left-y was right. They had made a special appearance at a Christmas concert and, at the end, announced that there would be a surprise this spring. Sometime during the spring, they would reveal to everyone another member of The Dangerous Four—her. Jamie still got chills thinking about it. Her, of all people. She was so lucky. That thought lifted her spirits some, and she found the strength to get back to practicing. They practiced a few more times, and then Left-y checked his watch.

"It's after midnight. I say we call it a night."

"Thank goodness," Jamie said as she collapsed onto a stool.

Once everything was put away, Rightey asked, "When's our next practice going to be?"

"Next year."

"That's a long time from now."

"Not really, only a few days. I say we take a break for a bit. Drummey, when's our next concert?"

"In a couple of weeks. There's a concert for bands in the area to help lift the winter blues. We've already got a spot."

"Great! We can keep performing and promote our little surprise," Left-y said as he looked at Jamie. She smiled despite her weariness.

"Then it's settled. We'll meet again for practice sometime in the new year. Let's go home."

"Great idea, Rousey," Left-y said, as the five of them left the clubhouse and headed for home.

CHAPTER 9

The band spent the rest of the winter and the beginning of spring teaching Jamie all of their songs as well as rehearsing. Jamie's sax blended well with the rest of the instruments to create a faster, jazzier sound. Drummey even composed a blues style song with a sax solo, just for Jamie. She really liked it. Drummey called it "Jam That Jazz," and it was just that—jamming.

Jamie finished the last few notes of her solo and ended in a bow. Left-y, Rightey, Rousey, and Drummey all applauded.

"Great job, Jamie," Left-y said.

"Yeah, that was awesome," Rightey added.

"Sounds like you know what you're doing," Rousey said.

"Thanks, guys, I've been working really hard on it," Jamie said as she breathed a little heavy. All the practicing on the sax had strengthened her lungs, but she was still a bit tired. She had plenty of energy left, though, and she would need it. The five of them had been rehearsing together for almost six months now, and they were well into spring. The Dangerous Four had played some concerts off and on throughout the winter, and they always ended by saying they had a surprise in the spring.

Now it was spring and time for the surprise. There had been a lot of promotion for this—a lot of anticipation. Now, finally, the night had come. Jamie was going to go onstage as one of The Dangerous Four. She carefully set her sax down in its case and looked at her reflection in it as it shined back. She had spent the last few nights polishing it and cleaning it up. Though there were a few bad spots, the sax practically shone like new. She smiled briefly and then began to get a little nervous, as she looked around the clubhouse. The other four members were all in their robes, and their masks were lying on the table. Jamie was still in her street clothes.

"Uh Left-y?"

"Yes?"

"What time is it?"

"About 6:30. Concert's in an hour. You ready?"

"Yeah. Actually, I was wondering what we were going to do about this?" She pointed to her street clothes. "I need a costume."

"Yes, you do," Left-y said as he went over to the table and picked up a box. He walked over to her. The others did as well.

Jamie's curiosity was peaked as Left-y held the box out to her. She opened it, and there inside was an old robe. Jamie reached in and pulled it out. She slid the old robe over her clothes. It looked just like the other ones, with different shades of purple and the many layers. It was a bit heavy, but it seemed to fit her well.

"This is great. I can move easily. Where did you find this?"

"In the old downtown junk store—where we got our robes and masks."

"Speaking of that, I'm still missing the most important part—my mask. I can't go on stage without my mask. I need it, and I need it now."

"You're right, Jamie; we wanted to wait until you were ready. Now that you are, we can give it to you. Look in the box."

Jamie looked, and there was her mask. It had all different shades of purple swirled around just like the robes. It looked kind of funny just lying in the box matted against the bottom. She didn't care, though. This was her mask, no one else's. That made it super cool. She took the mask out of the box and held it over her head. She looked at them with wide eyes as she slowly put it on. It fit perfectly. The material was soft against her face, and it wasn't really hot or stiff like Halloween masks. It moved easily with her facial muscles, especially around her mouth. She could easily play her sax.

"There's just one final thing left," Left-y said proudly. "We need to give you your stage name."

"I've been waiting for this."

"It was a hard decision," Left-y explained.

"Whoa, hold on a minute. You mean you've already decided what my name is? Don't I have a say in that?"

"Well Jamie, we just figured …"

"Figured what? That I couldn't come up with one? You guys all came up with your stage names. I want to pick mine too."

"OK, fine," Rousey said as he rolled his eyes. "What did you have in mind?"

"The Jazerae because I jam jazz on the sax."

"The Jazerae," Left-y said. The name did have a nice ring to it, and it did describe Jamie. Left-y, Rightey, Rousey, Drummey, and The Jazerae. That sounded good together, as if it was meant to be. Left-y looked at everyone.

"You all ready to go?"

They nodded.

"Great! Let's get going."

They made their way across town, and soon the five of them were backstage while their instruments were being set up. Left-y, Rightey, Rousey, and Drummey were laughing and joking around, while The Jazerae was walking nervously back and forth. She didn't know why, but all of a sudden her throat had gone dry, and her stomach began to hurt. She dropped to her knees and clutched her stomach.

"Oh, I don't feel well."

Left-y stopped laughing and went over to her. He looked at her and could see her arms shaking. He knelt down to her and asked, "Nervous, huh?"

"A little," she choked out. "I don't get it. I've been waiting for this moment for months. Now that it's finally here, I don't want to be here. I want to be somewhere else—anywhere but here."

"I know the feeling, Jazerae. All of us do. We all used to get really nervous right before we performed. You should have seen Drummey. His hands would sweat so badly, he could barely hold onto his drumsticks. I was scared to death to sing the first time. My throat would get so dry I couldn't even talk. It's normal, but the more you do it, the easier it will become."

"I hope so. I don't want to be nervous, but I want to be on the stage even more. I don't care if I throw up in front of everyone. I want to be on the stage!"

"Great!" Left-y said as he checked his watch. "It's almost show-time."

"Yes it is," came a voice from behind. They turned to find a tall, skinny guy with a headset and a clipboard in his left hand as he jotted down some notes. Left-y figured he must be a stagehand.

"Yeah, they're right here. Don't worry about it," he said into the headset. Then he turned to them. "Well, I guess have fun you … wait, one, two, three, four, five? There are five of you now?"

"Yes, there are," The Jazerae said proudly.

The stagehand shook his head and walked off. Everyone turned to Left-y.

"This is a very big night for all of us. We're going to be facing a lot of challenges. Let's hope the audience likes what they hear, but even if they don't, let's promise that we'll always be there for each other, no matter what. We'll always be friends."

"That's a great idea, Left-y," The Jazerae said as she looked around at the other four purple heads.

Left-y smiled and turned to Rousey. He could tell that Rousey was happy too. "So Rousey, what do you think?"

"I think," Rousey said through his smile, "that it's time the world met The Jazerae."

"Definitely. Well, you guys heard him. Let's make some tunes!"

With that the stagehand motioned for them and they ran onto the stage.

CHAPTER 10

The concert went better than Left-y could have imagined. Everybody loved The Jazerae, as well as The Dangerous Four's new style—though there had been a bit of confusion with the crowd at first. The audience didn't know what to make of the new sound, but by the end, everyone was cheering louder than ever before. The Dangerous Four relaxed a bit back at the clubhouse and talked about the night.

"What a rush!" The Jazerae exclaimed. "I can't believe it's over already. That was so much fun!"

"It definitely was," Left-y agreed. "Just wait till we do our next one."

"Oh, I can't wait. When's it going to be?"

"Don't really know, maybe in a couple of weeks. School's almost out, and we'll have a lot of time to rehearse and perform and all that."

"Yeah, we will," Drummey said, "but not tonight, it's too late."

"Yeah, it is," Left-y said as he yawned. He suddenly realized how tired he was.

"Hey, Drummey, do you think we'll perform a lot of concerts this summer?"

"Maybe a few, Jazerae. Why?"

"Well, I was just thinking. Doing concerts like we are now is fun, but what if we got a way to do a lot more and in different areas other than in town."

"How would we do that?"

"By getting someone to schedule them for us—to promote us, to manage us."

"You mean for us to get a manager?"

"Yeah, someone who really knows the music business. Someone who could get us gigs all over the place. Maybe even in the big city."

"You mean, in the Urbandome?"

"Yes."

All of them were silent for a moment. The Urbandome was where all the professional, big-time performers were. It made the Arena look tiny.

"There's no way we could play there," Rightey said. "That place is huge."

"Maybe, in time," Drummey said, thinking hard. "We can think about this for a bit. We've still got some time before the summer starts."

"How about we have a meeting the first night of summer?" Left-y suggested. "That would give us some time to think and give ourselves a break as well."

"Good idea, Left-y," Rousey said. "I could use a break."

"Right," Left-y said, as he opened the trap door, and they put their costumes away.

Then they cleaned up the clubhouse and headed for home. Rightey, Rousey, and Drummey hopped onto their bikes and disappeared off into the night, leaving Left-y and The Jazerae.

"This has been such a great night," The Jazerae said as she began to walk to her house.

"It sure was," Left-y agreed, as he grabbed his bike and walked it alongside her.

"You're really good."

"Thank you," The Jazerae said as she smiled. They continued on a bit, and then Left-y asked, "What are you going to do with the free time now? We've got about a week or so."

"Good question. One night, I'm going to invite Sarah over for fun. I've hardly done anything wither her since I joined."

"You know, you're right. I didn't think about it, but you don't sit with Sarah anymore at lunch or do as much stuff with her. You're not even around her hardly."

"Yeah, I know. I feel really bad. You and Rousey are lucky. You two can share The Dangerous Four, but I can't tell Sarah."

"That's got to be hard."

"It is, but you said I'd have to make some sacrifices if I wanted to do this, and I did."

They walked a little more until her house came into view. A few more steps, and they would be in her backyard.

"Well, I guess this is good night."

"Yeah, it is," The Jazerae said as she leaned over, and they hugged.

Neither one of them had planned it, but they both did it, and it felt good. They let go, and The Jazerae whispered, "Good night."

"Good night," Left-y replied as he sped away on his bike, leaving The Jazerae alone in the night.

◆　　◆　　◆

Several days passed, and one morning, the alarm clock rang. Jake shut if off quickly. He was happy it worked, but he was even more excited because it was now summer vacation.

Jake had been waiting for this day since school had started way back in September. Three whole months of no schoolwork, no getting up early, no boring teachers, and no Tone—just nice, long, hot days of relaxation under the sun. The only work he would have to do were some chores and, of course, his night job.

Now, if they could only finish "Liking You." They still had no way of ending the song, but he didn't let that get him down. He'd worry about that later. Right now, he had other things to do. He and Craig had planned to go to the pool that day. It had just opened, and they were ready for it. Unfortunately, the pool didn't open until the afternoon; he knew his mom would find something for him to do, and it wasn't going to be fun. Why was it that, when kids had nothing to do, parents thought they wanted to do chores? Didn't kids work hard enough at school? Didn't they deserve a break? Well, his parents didn't think so. Jake reluctantly stepped into the kitchen to receive his sentence.

It actually wasn't as bad as he thought. All he had to do was mow the lawn, and the grass needed it too. It was so long he could walk in it barefoot and not see his feet—not that he was barefoot. He had tried mowing the lawn barefoot once, and when he was done, his feet were completely dyed green. They'd stayed like that for a few days. He pushed the old, noisy mower along and finally finished the last little square of long grass.

"Whew!" had said as he shut off the mower and wiped the sweat from his forehead. He wondered how it had gotten so hot.

The pool would feel great after that chore. He checked his watch to find that the morning had gone by faster than he'd thought. He had just enough time to grab a quick lunch before his mom called him to get ready.

"Be right there, Mom," he called as he shoved the last bit of sandwich into his mouth and got ready for the pool.

His mom picked up Craig on the way, and by the look of it, Craig couldn't wait to get to the pool either.

The ride seemed to take forever, but at last they reached the public swimming pool. Jake and Craig had the door open before the car came to a stop.

"Have fun, boys. I'll pick you up at five o'clock, OK?"

"OK," they both said.

"And remember to put on lots of sunscreen."

"Sure, Mom," Jake said, rolling his eyes as he and Craig walked to the entrance. "She can be so annoying sometimes."

"At least she cares. Do you think my mom would have done this? All she ever does is fight with my dad."

"Things are still going rough, huh?" Jake said sympathetically. He really felt for Craig. For a while, his parents were getting along well. Now they had started fighting again. Jake didn't really know what else to say, so he made it sound sincere.

"Yeah, but I'm used to it. Look, it's the first day of summer vacation. We're here to have fun. Let's not think about any of our problems. Let's just have a good time."

"Fine with me," Jake said, as he stepped up to the counter to pay. Craig followed, and they went in.

Even though the pool had just opened, it was almost already filled. There were people jumping in from the sides, diving off the boards, and splashing everywhere he looked.

"Oh no, there's too many people here," Craig complained. "Let's go back."

"If you want to, have fun by yourself then," Jake said as he spotted a patch of green grass and went over to it. It was just big enough for the two of them, and it was practically the only patch of grass left in the entire place.

"Hey, wait for me," Craig yelled after him. He sat his towel down next to Jake's just in time.

"Man this place is crowded," he said as he looked around. "I bet you could find just about anyone here."

"Yeah you could, and I just did. Look."

Craig looked over in the direction Jake was pointing, and sure enough, there stood Nick.

"Hey, Nick, what are you doing here?" Jake called.

"I could ask you the same question."

"Is Ryan with you?"

"He's already in the pool."

"Well, I say we join him!"

"Sounds good to me," Craig said, as the three of them got to the edge of the pool and jumped in. Whoa! That water was cold! But it sure felt good on such a hot day.

"Wow, this is great!" Jake exclaimed as he hopped around trying to warm up. After a few minutes he had gotten used to the water, and he could go under easily. He called out to Ryan, "I wonder if anyone else we know is here?"

"Actually, Jake, there is," Ryan said with a smile, "and she's right over there."

Jake looked over out of the pool and saw Jamie sunbathing on a pink towel. Summer had just started, and she was already getting a good tan.

"Well don't just stand there and stare; go say hi."

Jake decided to take Ryan's advice. He got out of the pool and headed toward her. He leaned over and was about to say hi when he realized she was asleep.

"Aren't you going to say something?" Craig asked.

"No good; she's asleep."

"Well then, I guess we'll just have to wake her up."

Craig got out of the pool and leaned back over the water. He cupped his hands and filled them. He walked over and held his hands over Jamie's head.

"Craig, don't do that. She doesn't deserve it."

"Maybe not, but it'll be funny," Craig said as he splashed the water onto Jamie's face.

"Agh!!!"

Jamie jumped up and shook her head.

"All right, all right. Who did this to me?" she demanded in an angry voice.

"Uh, Jake did!" Craig blurted out.

"What? Me! Why would I do something like that?"

"Just tell me the truth, Jakey. Did you, or did you not do it?"

As Jake looked straight into her dark, brown eyes, he knew she meant business. He could tell she trusted him to tell the truth. He almost never told lies to anyone, but at that moment, he would never have lied to her.

"Who are you going to believe, me or Craig?"

"You do have a good point there," she said with a smile. Jake could tell that her mood had changed but changed to what, he didn't know.

"I know exactly who to believe now, Craig."

"You what?" Jake said surprised. Now he was really confused.

"You want me to think that Craig did it so I would throw him in the pool, but I'm onto your little game here. You're not as smooth as you think. I hope you like the water."

"I'm going to regret this, but why?"

"Because you're going to go for a little swim with me, OK?"

"Nice try, Jamie, but it's break right now. We can't go in the pool."

Jamie bit her lower lip.

"Darn it, after the break then."

"Now I'm really scared," Jake said sarcastically as he went back to his towel.

"So, what's going on?" Craig asked.

"Oh nothing; just that now, because of you, Jamie wants to throw me into the pool."

"You're going to let Jamie push you around? Tone I can understand, but Jamie?"

"Relax. I don't think she was serious when she said she'd do it, and even if she does try to throw me in the pool, I won't let her."

"Well, you'd better tell her that because the break's almost over."

Just then a voice came on over the intercom: "The break is over. You may now swim."

"Well, here she comes."

Jamie walked over between Jake and the pool. She motioned for him to get in.

"Aw, but I don't want to. I'm all dried off," he complained.

"Too bad. You're going in, and that's final."

Jamie grabbed his arm and threw him into the pool. Actually, Jake jumped when she pulled, so it just looked like she threw him. The water was even colder than before.

"Brrrrr! Hey, Jamie, how about helping me out?"

"OK, Jakey, you really do look cold," she said as she extended her hand. He took it, but instead of pulling himself up, he pulled her in.

"Ah! You punk, what was that for?"

"Hey, you got me wet, so I got you wet. Now we're even."

"Fine, I suppose so, but it wasn't very funny."

"Yes, it was," Jake said with a smile. Then he became serious. "Can you meet tonight?"

"Yeah sure. I can make it."

"Great, see you then," Jake said as he swam over to Craig in the deep end. Jamie wasn't very fond of deep swimming, so she decided to get back to sunbathing.

She lay down on her towel and closed her eyes but was interrupted only a few seconds later by a familiar voice: "So, there you are."

Jamie opened her eyes and saw Sarah standing over her.

"Oh, hey Sarah, having fun? I didn't know you were here."

"Big surprise. I've been here the whole time. Not like you'd care."

Jamie was a little confused. Sarah seemed to be upset with her, but she didn't know why. She sat up and looked at her.

"Sarah, what's wrong?"

"I can't believe you didn't know I was here."

"I was sunbathing and had my eyes closed, OK? I just didn't see you."

"But you sure saw Jake and everyone else. How is your boyfriend anyway?"

"Fine, I guess, but he's not really my boyfriend yet."

"Oh, will you stop it already, Jamie. Just drop the act and admit it."

"Admit what?"

"That you're boy crazy."

"What?"

"You're boy crazy, and you know it. You only moved when you saw him."

"He talked to me, and if I'd have known you were here, I'd have said hi to you. I don't see why you're so upset with me. You were fine at the sleepover last weekend."

"You think us hanging out once a month and you spending all your other time with them is fine? Jamie, what's happening to you? You can't even admit that you're obsessed with boys now, and you lied to me."

"What do you mean I lied to you?" Jamie said as she got to her feet.

"You say Jake isn't your boyfriend? I overheard you two planning a meeting tonight. You lied right to my face!"

"Sarah, it isn't like that."

"Really? Then what's it like?"

"It's complicated. I wish I could tell you; I really do."

Sarah shook her head. "You know what, if you want to keep secrets, fine. I've got some secrets of my own. You might not be the only girl for Jake."

Jamie crossed her arms and looked down at Sarah. "Who else would be interested? You? Ha! You wouldn't have a chance. Don't be mad at me because boys like me and not you!"

Jamie put her hands over her mouth. Did she just say that? She couldn't believe it. She saw Sarah's lower lip quiver a bit, and her eyes began to fill with tears.

"Sarah, I'm so sorry. I didn't mean it."

"No, no you did, and if that's how you feel; fine. If you want Jake, or any of those other boys as your friends, you can have them, because those are the only friends you're going to have!"

Sarah pushed by Jamie and ran off. Jamie could tell that she was trying to keep from crying in front of her.

"Sarah, wait, please! I'm sorry, I'm sorry," she said quieter the second time. What had she done? She couldn't believe she'd just yelled at her best friend like that.

Did Sarah mean what she said? Did she have a crush on Jake? Jamie thought Sarah liked Craig. No, wait, Sarah liked Rousey. Maybe she thought Jake was Rousey? It was all too confusing. Jamie laid back down on her towel and began to sunbathe again. Why was this so hard? It seemed like she had to choose between Sarah and Jake, but she didn't want to choose. Jamie decided to take a quick nap and get a tan as well. At least some good would come out of this.

CHAPTER 11

"I can't believe it's eleven-thirty and The Jazerae isn't here yet," Left-y said as he paced around the clubhouse. "Where could she be?"

"Will you relax, Left-y? I'm sure she'll be here any minute."

"I hope you're right, Rightey."

"Of course I'm right. There she is."

Left-y turned to find The Jazerae standing in the doorway, a little out of breath.

"Sorry if I'm late, guys. My parents almost caught me sneaking out. I had to wait for things to quiet down, and it took forever. I ran here all the way."

"You don't have to worry about excuses, Jazerae. What's important is that you're here now."

"Aw, thanks Left-y, I knew you'd understand," she said as she smiled at him.

Rousey made a face.

"So, what's on the agenda for tonight?"

"Yeah, what are we doing?" Rousey asked. "Practicing our songs? Listening to music?"

"We're going to figure out what to do for the summer," Drummey said as he looked at The Jazerae. "I liked your idea about getting us a manager. That would really help us. I think it's time we take this thing to the next level."

"What do you mean?"

"I mean do a tour."

The four of them looked at Drummey and smiled. All of them liked the idea.

"It would be a small tour, of course," he said to clarify, "just around the area and to neighboring towns, but we could build up our name, and then, who knows?"

"I like it," Left-y said. "Besides, we've really done everything we can do on our own. Now, who would want to manage us?"

All of them thought for awhile, and then suddenly The Jazerae jumped up and said, "That's it! I know exactly who could manage us."

"Who?" they all asked.

"My uncle, Mike, of course. Why didn't I think of him before? He's already in the music business, and I know he loves live bands. I think he's even mentioned something about wanting to manage a band awhile back. He'd be perfect!"

"Uh, maybe," Left-y said hesitantly. It was obvious he'd forgotten to mention to her that Mike had tried to scam The Dangerous Four before and failed miserably. Since then, they really hadn't gotten along. Left-y decided he'd better tell her.

"Uh, Jazerae, there's something we need to tell you about your uncle."

"What is it, Left-y?"

"You uncle isn't exactly the type of guy you think he is."

The Jazerae became confused and narrowed her eyes. "What are you getting at?"

"What I mean is …"

"He's a crook; tried to scam us out of our own concert. We found out and stopped him; now he doesn't like us," Rousey said quickly.

"What?" The Jazerae said surprised and a little angered.

"I was getting to that," Left-y said. "Jazerae, do you remember when we headlined our first concert?"

"You mean the Halloween one?"

"No, before that, the one where I signed your CD."

"Oh, yeah!"

"Well, it turns out that that concert wasn't meant for us at all."

"I don't understand."

"Mike had hired another band to dress like us and pretend to be us. We just thought he had really wanted us to come, but when we saw what he was up to, we had to act. We got rid of The Fake Four and took their place. We confronted Mike afterward, and he was not happy about it."

"You're telling me that my uncle is a crook, and you expect me to believe that?" The Jazerae said as her breathing became short and detached. It was the type of breathing someone does before they cry. Left-y could tell she was getting upset, and that she was trying to control it. He understood how she felt. This was her uncle they were talking about. Left-y wasn't scared of her going on a rampage, but he motioned for Rousey to block the door.

"We don't know for sure, but it does seem that way. All we know is that he doesn't take us seriously."

The Jazerae was silent for a few moments. "What group?"

"Huh?"

"What group did he have dress up as you guys?"

"The Rat Tails."

The Jazerae looked at him for a long time. Finally she said, "I don't believe you."

"Jazerae, I know it's hard to believe that your uncle would do this, but he did."

"No, Left-y, it doesn't make sense."

"What do you mean?"

"He hates The Rat Tails."

"He does?" all of them asked in amazement.

"Yeah, he can't stand them. He's told me several times."

"Then why did he have them impersonate us?"

"I don't know. Look, you guys can say what you want, but I don't care. Maybe there's something we don't understand?"

"He made it pretty clear to us," Rousey said.

"I'm not sure about that," Left-y said.

"What do you mean?" Rousey asked.

"Right after we won The Costumed Battle of the Bands, Mike came up to me and said we deserved to win. It may have been my imagination, but I swear he even smiled."

"Well, then we've got to find out now. I'm going to talk to him as The Jazerae and get the honest truth."

"OK," Left-y said. "If you've got to do this, go, but I'm going with you."

"I was hoping you would."

"Great, but there's just one problem," Rightey said. "When are you going to see him?"

"You guys can go late tomorrow night. He does a segment in the middle of the night."

"Right!" The Jazerae said excited. "It's from midnight to 4:00 am. He started doing that for some extra cash."

"So it's settled. You two will go over there to get the truth."

"You got it, Rousey."

"Great. So, what are we going to do till then?"

Left-y looked at his watch.

"Well, we've still got some time before midnight. I say we practice a bit."

"I'm up for that," Rightey said.

"Yeah," they all agreed.

"Well, let's not waste any more time. Let's make some tunes!"

◆   ◆   ◆

Even though the practice was short, Left-y thought it went well. Everyone left feeling good about the plan. Left-y and The Jazerae were a little nervous about what was ahead. They both counted down the hours until the next night came. They had planned to meet in front of The Jazerae's house at two. It was ten after two, and Left-y was nowhere in sight. The Jazerae was beginning to worry. It wasn't like him to be late. She squinted hard and saw a figure moving quickly toward her. A couple of minutes later, Left-y rode up to her.

"I was wondering when you'd get here," she said.

"I know. I'm sorry. I had to make sure I wouldn't wake my parents. Ready?"

"Ready."

They sped off for the radio station. The streets were very dark, except for the little patches of light the streetlights made. They had to make sure they avoided the light, in case someone was watching. Left-y was getting tired, weaving around all the patches of light, but at last they made it to the station. Both of them slowed down and silently put their bikes down behind a bush.

"How will we get in?" Left-y asked.

The Jazerae tried the door, and it opened. "We walk in," she said smiling.

Left-y rolled his eyes, and they entered. They looked around a bit, but no one could be found. There were only a couple of very dim lights down the hall and no sound. The place was empty.

"No sign of Mike, or anyone," The Jazerae said. "Are you sure this is the right place?"

"Positive. Maybe he's on another floor. Let's go." Left-y led the way to some stairs. "Let's go down. I think I see a light."

They went down the stairs and found out that the light was just a security light, but they had made the right choice. There was a door that led to the radio station.

"This is it," Left-y said as he tried the door. It opened easily, and they went in.

The place was a little different than the floor above them. There were a few more lights on and a couple of people here and there. Left-y and The Jazerae sneaked past them when they weren't looking. It was a little difficult running in their robes, but they managed to pull it off. They didn't want anyone knowing they were there except Mike. Now if only they could find him.

"Where would he be?" Left-y asked in a whisper.

"Probably in the studio," The Jazerae whispered back. "I think they're over there."

They made a mad dash down the hall, turned a corner, went down another one, and found doors to two different studios.

"Oh no," Left-y said. "Which one do we pick?"

The Jazerae didn't get a chance to answer. They heard footsteps coming toward them. They looked around. The hall was bare except for a big plant a couple of doors down.

"Quick, hide!" Left-y hissed as they both ran to the other side of the plant and pressed themselves against the wall.

Left-y thought for sure that whoever it was would see them, as a shadow appeared across the hall. The figure rounded the corner, and it was Mike. He seemed to be in a very big hurry as he stuffed what appeared to be a sandwich into his mouth and went into one of the studios.

"Well, that makes it easy," The Jazerae said.

"I can't believe he didn't notice us," Left-y said, as he went over to the door. "This is it. No turning back now."

The Jazerae nodded.

Left-y opened the door, and they both went in.

The studio was actually pretty small. There was equipment of all types up against one wall, with buttons and blinking lights. There were also a lot of dials and switches. Mike was behind a small counter talking into a mic. He was so into his broadcast, he didn't notice them right away. His eyes finally wandered toward them, and he nearly jumped out of his chair. He stared at them for a few seconds, forgetting that he was on the air, but he finally collected himself and said, "I've got to take a break, but I'll be right back."

He flipped a switch that Left-y figured played commercials. Mike got out of his chair, leaned over the counter, and stared at them. Then he asked, "Who are you?"

"Don't you recognize us?" Left-y said smoothly. I'm Left-y, and this is The Jazerae."

"Sure you are," he said sarcastically. "I don't know how you got in here, but I don't have time for jokes. Now, if you'll excuse me, I've got a radio show to do."

"We're not going anywhere until we get some answers," Left-y said in a firmer voice.

"Just a sec," Mike said as he flipped a couple of switches. "There are some songs playing now. I only have a few minutes. So, what do the two of you want?"

"The truth," Left-y said plainly.

"The truth about what?"

"About the night you got The Rat Tails to pretend to be us, and we crashed the concert. You remember that, don't you?"

"Yeah, I remember it. Look, you guys don't know the whole story."

"Then tell us."

"OK," Mike said as he leaned over to them and said in a hushed voice, "Off the record, and just between you and me, here's what really happened. My boss told me that The Rat Tails wanted to give a tribute performance to you guys. They needed someone to arrange it. My boss nominated me for the job without ever asking me. I couldn't say no; this was my boss. I'm not much of a fan of The Rat Tails, but I figured it wouldn't be that bad. Then I heard them sing—Jeff with that annoying voice; and the fact that they were all right-handed didn't help either. That's why it was decided that they would lip-sync to your songs. I had no idea they wanted to take your name or anything like that."

Mike went back over to the control panel and flipped a few switches. He talked for a bit while Left-y and The Jazerae sat there and thought about what he'd said. Lefty was beginning to think Mike wasn't such a bad guy after all. He sure didn't sound as mean as when The Dangerous Four had confronted him at the concert.

Mike finished talking and turned back to them. "I really didn't want to do it, Left-y."

"It sounds like you didn't have a choice."

"I didn't. You know the only reason why I play their songs is that my boss makes me."

"Why would your boss make you play them?"

"Because my boss happens to be the mother of the lead singer."

"You mean Jeff's mom is your boss?"

"Exactly."

"I guess it's true. It's not what, but who you know that counts."

Mike gave a chuckle.

"Personally, I think you guys are ten times better than The Rat Tails. They just have someone who can get them places, and you don't."

"We know. That's part of the reason we're here."

"What do you mean?"

"The five of us have taken The Dangerous Four as far as we can go. We're looking for someone who can help us out—someone who knows the business and can get us into places we can't. We're looking for a manager."

Mike straightened up. "Do you want me to find you a manager?"

"Actually, we were hoping you'd be our manager," The Jazerae said.

Mike sat back in his chair and was silent for awhile. Both Left-y and The Jazerae could tell he was processing this very hard. Finally, he spoke: "What makes you think I would want to manage a group, especially a group of kids?"

"It's always been your dream to manage a group," The Jazerae blurted out, but she was sorry she did.

"How did you know that?"

"Uh, that's what I've heard at least."

"Well, it doesn't matter how you found out. You're right. That is something I've always wanted to do. Imagine—me, the manager of The Dangerous Four. Now, I know you guys aren't crazy about the money, but how would that work?"

"You wouldn't have to quit this job, and if there was a contract, I think we could work out the money issues."

"Sounds great. I do another late-night show in a couple of days. Why don't you meet me here around eleven, and we'll work out the details then; deal?"

Left-y stood up and shook Mike's hand. "Deal. That will give us some time to talk things over."

"Completely understandable."

"You won't regret this, Mike," The Jazerae said, as she got up and they headed to the door.

"I don't think I will. Now, if you two will excuse me, I have a show to do."

Mike went back to his chair, flipped a switch, and waved good-bye as he began to speak into the mic. Left-y and The Jazerae walked out of the studio and dodged anyone who might have given them trouble. They both raced up the flight of stairs and onto the dark, quiet floor.

"That went pretty smooth," Left-y said.

"Yeah, see! I told you he wasn't a bad guy."

"Yeah, you were right."

"As always."

"We can celebrate later. Now we have to get back."

They walked out the front door and found their bikes. As they rode back to the clubhouse, Left-y couldn't believe how fortunate they had been. Mike was really going to do it. They had found themselves a manager. Both Left-y and The Jazerae knew that things were really going to change for them. They just had no idea how.

CHAPTER 12

Left-y and The Jazerae were right. Having a manager really changed things. They met with him off and on through June. Mike got them gigs three to four nights a week in town and the surrounding area. On the nights they weren't performing, they were practicing in the clubhouse.

Although Mike was their manager, The Dangerous Four never told him about the clubhouse. Whenever they had a meeting, they would meet him in his studio late at night, as well as for the gigs. All five of them really liked him a lot. It was hard to believe that they'd thought the same guy had tried to scam them less than a year ago. Now he was the coolest guy they knew. Maybe it was the fact that he was in his early twenties and still acted like a kid sometimes, but whatever the reason, they completely trusted him as their manager. Of course, they did keep a few secrets, such as their real identities.

Things were really looking good for The Dangerous Four. It was the Fourth of July, and Left-y had called them all out to the clubhouse.

"So, why'd you call a meeting tonight?" Rightey asked.

"Isn't it obvious? Check it out!"

The five of them looked across the empty field, and off in the distance, fireworks went off and exploded in the sky and then faded into the night.

"Great idea, Left-y!" Rousey said as he hopped onto the roof of the clubhouse.

"Hey, you can see better up here. Come on up!"

They went over to the clubhouse. Left-y helped The Jazerae up, and soon, all of them were enjoying the fireworks. They were going off all around them. Some whistled as they flew up, while others exploded with a loud bang! They watched them all for quite awhile, until Rousey began to doze and almost fell off the roof.

"Whoa, that was close. Man, I'm getting tired. What time is it?"

"It's only eleven-thirty."

"Really? I don't know why I'm so tired."

"Maybe it's because you were so busy doing stuff all day," Rightey said with a yawn. "I'm tired too."

"I'm worn out as well," Drummey said.

"Is everyone going to leave?" The Jazerae asked.

"I could stay for a bit," Left-y offered.

"Great, because I'm not the least bit tired."

"That works. You two can watch the fireworks together while the rest of us go home and get some sleep," Rightey said, as he jumped off the roof and went over to his bike.

Rousey and Drummey did the same, and soon Left-y and The Jazerae were left alone on the roof of the clubhouse. The Jazerae laid down and stared up at the cloudless sky. All the stars shown and made beautiful designs. As The Jazerae traced them out with her finger, Left-y's voice interrupted her thoughts, "What a perfect night for this."

"That's for sure."

"The only thing that would make it better is if we could see them closer, maybe if we were higher up too."

"How could we get higher up?"

"We could be at the Peak."

"The Peak?" she asked as she sat up. "But that's clear across town. We'd never make it on our bikes. Even by car, it would take a while, and we can't drive."

"Calm down, Jazerae. I wasn't serious. The only way we'd make it in time is if, I don't know, we could magically fly over there."

"We can't do that either," The Jazerae said as she shifted her weight. "Hey, can we do one thing?"

"What?"

"We're not at a practice or performing, so can we drop the stage names for the night?"

"Sure thing, Jamie," Jake said as a big, green, star firework exploded, followed by a loud bang. As Jake watched the fireworks, his thoughts drifted back over the year, and he remembered something Jamie had said. "Hey Jamie, do you remember back last fall when Tone was after me but left you alone?"

"Yeah, I remember that."

"Why did he leave you alone?"

"I suppose I can tell you. He was giving me a hard time once, but I wouldn't take it, so I fought back."

"You punched him?"

"No, I kicked him, in the nuts."

Jake swallowed and crossed his legs.

Jamie gave a giggle. "Oh relax, Jake. Besides, it couldn't have hurt that much."

"Want to bet? You have no idea what that feels like. No wonder he left you alone after that."

"Yeah, hasn't bothered me since," Jamie said, and then she sighed and looked a little sad.

"What is it?"

"What is what?"

"That look. You've been giving that look off and on for the past month. You seem really sad sometimes."

"I was just thinking about the past month and how busy we've been. Mike has really been working us. Don't get me wrong; I love having him as our manager, but we've been performing three to four concerts a week, and the times when we're not on the stage, we're practicing. I'm surprised we had today off to be honest."

"Yeah, I know what you mean. It seems like our whole life is The Dangerous Four. We don't have any time to play anymore. You're right, Mike is an awesome manager. I like how he kind of gave us a nickname."

"What do you mean?"

"That article the paper wrote about us a couple of weeks ago. Mike said we were like 'musicians in the night.'"

"That's right, he did, and it's true. We really are 'musicians in the night.'"

"Yeah, that's cool."

They both watched some more fireworks. After a bit Jamie said, "Jake, since you honestly trust me, I can trust you too. You were right when you say that I've been sad, but I haven't been completely honest with you."

"You haven't?"

"Sort of. When I told you that I didn't like being so busy, that was true, but there's more than that."

"Does this have anything to do with your friends?"

"Yeah, with me and Sarah. You see, about a month ago when I saw you at the pool, after you left, I ran into Sarah, and we had a fight."

"OK, but friends fight."

"Not like this. I said something to her."

"What did you say?"

"Something really mean and completely untrue," Jamie said sadly as she closed her eyes. Then she slapped her knee. "I wish I hadn't said it!"

"Did you try apologizing?"

"Yeah, I must have called her half a dozen times, but she won't talk to me."

"For a month? You must have really hurt her."

"Yeah, and it hurts me too," she said as she turned to Jake. She was trying hard to keep from crying. "You see, the truth is, I don't have many friends. Sarah was one of the very few real friends I had, and now we're not friends anymore."

"That doesn't make sense. You were always hanging around other friends."

"Those girls are Sarah's friends. I know them, but they're not my friends. Jake, you don't know how many times I've wished I could tell Sarah that I was one of The Dangerous Four. Then she'd understand. You are so lucky, you know that? You and Craig are best friends, and you can do this together, but not me and Sarah."

Jake didn't know what to say. He had no idea Jamie felt like this. Then a thought came to him. "Was the fight the only reason you two aren't friends anymore?"

"Well, she did say we don't do anything together, but if she knew, she'd understand."

"Think so?"

"What do you mean?"

"Well, you'd still be busy with The Dangerous Four. You still wouldn't have any time to do anything with her. She would just know you were performing or practicing instead of hanging out with her. You two may have fought anyway."

Jamie looked at him oddly and thought it through. "You know, you're probably right. I never even thought of that. Wow, I remember when I wanted to join, and you guys were trying to talk me out of it; you said there was a lot of work and sacrifices to this whole musician thing. I guess this is what you were talking about. I knew I'd have to give up a lot of my free time, but I never thought I'd have to give up my friends."

"Jamie, you don't have to give up your friends. Maybe Sarah just needs a lot of time, and when the time is right, she'll forgive you, and you two can be friends again," Jake said as he gave her a hug.

"Thank you, Jake. That means a lot," Jamie said, as Jake let go and they looked into each other's eyes.

Jake still had his hands on her shoulders. He gave a slight smile, and they both slowly began to lean in. Jamie's heart began to pound harder and faster as she realized what was happening. They were going to kiss. This was going to be her first kiss, and it had to be perfect.

Jamie leaned in too and was ready for the kiss when she felt the worst feeling she could have imagined at the time. A mosquito had landed on her cheek and was ready to bite. She fought the temptation to swat it as long as she could, but it bit her and she couldn't stand it.

"Agh!" she said as she slapped her cheek and bumped Jake's head in the process.

"Ouch!"

"I'm sorry!" Jamie pleaded. "I didn't mean to, honest!"

"I'm sure you didn't," Jake said as he rubbed his head. "Maybe we should hold off on that for a bit."

"Yeah, maybe," Jamie said as she turned away. How could she have done that? She had liked Jake for so long; he'd finally made his move, and she'd blown it. Although it could have been worse—she could have slapped him instead.

They both continued to watch the fireworks for a little longer, and then Jamie gave a shudder.

"Cold?"

"A little," she said as she gave a yawn.

"It is getting late," Jake said. "Maybe we should go home."

"Yeah, I guess so," Jamie said sadly.

She hopped down off the clubhouse, and Jake followed. Jake grabbed his bike, and they walked through the field.

When they reached her backyard, Jamie turned to face Jake. The wind ran through his hair and ruffled it. A few fireworks went off in the distance.

"Jake."

"Yes?"

"Thanks for watching the fireworks with me."

"You're welcome," he said as he started to ride away, but Jamie grabbed his arm.

"Wait. Uh before, and we were going to … and I slapped my cheek."

"Yeah?"

"You know, I wanted to."

"Yes, I know. Maybe later," he said as he looked at her. The moon shone behind him and cast down on them. Jamie seemed almost to be glowing in the moonlight. He put his arms around her and hugged her good night.

He gave her a quick peck on the cheek and peddled off into the night. Jamie put her hand on her cheek where Jake had kissed her. It wasn't exactly what she was hoping for, but it was a start.

CHAPTER 13

A couple of weeks passed, and The Dangerous Four found themselves working on their songs, preparing for their next concert. Left-y had just finished tuning his guitar when Rightey asked when they'd be performing.

"Wednesday, Rightey," he replied. "We should practice tonight since it's in a couple of days."

"Every concert's within a couple of days," Rousey complained.

"I know," Rightey agreed. "It's like we don't have any free time anymore, and we're on summer vacation."

"Just imagine what it would be like if we were in school."

"Ugh, I don't even want to think about that, Left-y," The Jazerae said as she shuddered.

"Yeah, tell me about it," Rousey said. "And this year is going to be really weird. We're starting middle school."

He was right. In about a month, all of them would be going into middle school. That meant a new school, new teachers, and new kids. It was kind of scary, but they didn't want to think about it now. They had work to do.

"You guys tuned up and ready to go?" Left-y asked.

They all nodded.

"Let's make some tunes!"

◆　　◆　　◆

The practice went well, and so did the concert. The audience had really seemed to like them. By the end, they were chanting for an encore, but The Dangerous Four were out of songs. Mike suggested that they come up with some more, and Left-y agreed. Drummey got to work, and the rest of the summer was spent on new songs, as well as doing more concerts. Every night, they practiced or performed, and even though they were getting tired, they all noticed they were getting better and better. Drummey's new songs challenged each of them, but they were up to it and made them work. Left-y could feel the new calluses on his fingers from playing so much, but he didn't mind. He liked the fact that he had some kind of badge to show for his work.

The days were beginning to get shorter as the last bit of summer faded away, and before he knew it, it was time for school to start again. Jake had already been shopping for school supplies and new clothes. He didn't see why he had to get new clothes to start school. They'd just get dirty anyway. He had been on a tour of the school the week before, but he was still nervous. He couldn't believe how different middle school was. He didn't keep all his stuff in his desk, but in a locker. He tried to work the combination, but it wouldn't open. Jake wasn't worried; he'd figure it out later. Jake did like the idea of moving around from class to class. It got so boring staring at the same thing sometimes. The only thing he really hated was not having recess anymore. How did people survive without recess?

He stood anxiously at the bus stop. His mom had wanted to give him a ride, but he'd insisted on taking the bus. He looked around at the other kids. They seemed so much older and bigger than him. He hoped he was in the right place and was relieved when Craig came up to him.

"What are you doing here?"

"Taking the bus," Craig responded.

"Since when do you take the bus?"

"Since my mom decided to get a job."

"She did?"

"Yeah, said she needed a change and wanted to break free, whatever that means."

Jake shrugged his shoulders. The bus came, and they got on and headed for school.

The morning was exciting and dull at the same time. Jake was excited to be in the new school with so many other kids, but it was also boring because it was the first day. He talked to the others about their schedules and found that Craig was in his first class, Nick, his third, Ryan, his seventh, and Jamie, his last. The coolest part was they all had lunch together. He joined Nick and Craig in the lunch line, which took forever. When they finally got their food, they looked around for a place to sit. They spotted Ryan at a nearby table.

"Is the food any good?" Craig asked.

"I wouldn't say good," Ryan said between mouthfuls. "It's about the same as in our old school."

"Yuck!" Craig said and made a face. He hated school food, but he started to eat it anyway. Jake and Nick did the same. Jamie joined them soon after.

"Anyone's morning fun?" Jake asked.

Nick gave him a strange look. "It's the first day of school. How could that be fun? Although I did hear something about sixth grade sports. That might be cool."

"I didn't know you were into sports," Ryan said.

"I'm not really, but I've always liked football. Maybe I can get into that. If I have time, of course."

"Of course," they all said, and they all knew what he meant.

"Not that I'm complaining or anything; besides, I'd probably get beaten out anyway by some of the other kids. Have you seen some of the kids here?"

"Yeah, tell me about it," Ryan said as he gulped down the last of his milk. "Some of these guys are huge. I went into the bathroom this morning, and I swear I saw a guy in there shaving."

"Are you sure he wasn't turning into a werewolf?"

"Yeah, I'm sure of that, Craig."

"You think the guys are bad; you should see what goes on in the girls' bathroom."

"And what goes on in there?"

Jamie stared at Craig. "You wouldn't want to know."

"OK, enough about this. Let's talk about something important, like our next meeting."

"And when would that be, Jake?"

"In a couple of nights, Craig. There's a few things I want to talk to Mike about."

"Like what?"

Jake didn't get a chance to answer. The bell rang, and they got up to leave.

"I'll tell you guys later," Jake said, as he hurried off to his afternoon classes.

Jamie sped down the street on her bike as she rode home. Her backpack shifted every time she peddled. She didn't normally ride her bike to school, but it was nice out and she wanted to give it a try. She went up her driveway and looked in the garage as she got off her bike. She saw her dad's car, which was strange because he should still be at work. She wondered why he was home early. She went inside and set her backpack down.

"I'm home."

"We're in the kitchen, dear. Come up here."

Jamie went into the kitchen and found both her parents sitting at the table. Her mom smiled at her. "Hi, sweetie, how was school?"

"It was all right. There are a lot of new kids there."

"I'm sure there are. Uh, your father and I have some exciting news for you. Take a seat."

Jamie sat down and looked confused.

"How come you're home early, Dad? Just what is this exciting news?"

CHAPTER 14

Left-y spent the next few days talking things over with Mike and was ready to tell the others. Rightey and Rousey were setting up and tuning their guitars. Drummey was bent over at the table examining the music of "Liking You."

"I still don't get it," he told Left-y. "I keep trying different endings, but nothing seems to sound right. I'm running out of ideas on what to do."

"Maybe we should just stick something on the end."

"No, Rousey, we want this to sound good," Left-y said as he got out his guitar. "Besides, we don't want to rush it and get a better idea later on. We should work on the songs that are done now."

"But we can't do that without The Jazerae," Rightey said. "Where is she?"

"Yeah, it's not like her to be late. I hope she's OK."

"I'm fine, Left-y," The Jazerae said, as she walked in. Left-y got her sax, and she began to set up.

"I almost fell asleep waiting up. That's why I'm a little late."

"At least you're here now," Drummey said as he went over to his drums. "Now Left-y can tell us the big news."

"What big news?" The Jazerae asked nervously.

"The big news that I've been discussing with Mike. It won't be for a bit, but he liked the idea of us playing in the Urbandome, and he thinks he can get us in."

All four of them went wide-eyed.

"No way!" exclaimed Rightey.

"Oh yes!" Left-y yelled back.

"When?"

"In about six weeks, mid-October. There's a big weekend concert with a bunch of other acts. We'll have a performance all our own."

"This is great!" yelled The Jazerae.

"We'll be famous," Rousey said with a smile.

"And we'll be with all the pros," The Jazerae said, "all the big acts, and in the big city. This is fantastic! When did you say it was?"

"Mid-October."

"No! We've got to do it sooner. I don't have that much time."

"What do you mean?" Left-y asked.

"Uh, I mean, I don't want to wait; that's all. I don't have that much time to wait. Don't you guys want to do it now?"

"Yeah, but were going to need to practice a lot more if we're going to play at the Urbandome."

"You're right, Rightey. Mike feels the same way. We're going to need to practice more often and for longer. We'll meet at 11:00 and go till 12:30 almost every night."

"Almost every night! Are you kidding?"

"No, we've got to work harder if were going to do this."

Rightey shook his head. "This is getting out of control. We've been practicing more and more. We're better than we've ever been, and it's still not enough. We don't have any free time anymore."

"I know what you mean," Drummey said as he twirled his drumstick. "I've heard some of our teachers may be giving us homework this year. When are we supposed to do that if we're practicing all the time?"

"But we've had the whole summer off."

"Not really, Left-y," Rightey said. "We practiced all the time too. Now we're practicing more. Let's face it. The Dangerous Four is our life now. Before we were just having fun; but now we have to do it."

"Are you saying you don't want to do this anymore?" Left-y asked in surprise.

Rightey paced a bit and shook his head. "I … I don't know what I'm saying. All I know is that there is other stuff I want to try, and I can't do it because of The Dangerous Four. But that doesn't mean I want to quit."

"Do you want to play at the Urbandome?"

"Yeah, I really want to."

"Then let's practice up till then and go from there. Honestly, I'm getting tired of practicing all the time too. It's nice to know I'm not the only one."

"But you're right, Left-y," Rousey said. "If we're going to play with the big acts, we're going to need the practice."

"Then let's get going," Left-y said, as he picked up his guitar. "Let's make some tunes!"

The Dangerous Four practiced hard that night. They practiced so hard they were all sweating by the time they were done. They put their instruments away and were getting ready to leave when The Jazerae went over to Left-y.

"Great practice tonight."

"Yeah, I'll say so. You sound really good on your sax."

"Thanks, I've been practicing all summer long. I wish I could show Sarah ..." Her voice trailed off.

"You two still not talking?"

"No, I've tried to apologize, but every time I say I'm busy, she gets mad. I can't tell her about this, so we just end up in a fight."

"Have you seen her around school?"

"Yeah, but just in the hall. She was walking with Kayla and some other girls. She's got new friends," she said with a sigh.

"I'm sorry, Jazerae."

"Yeah, me too." Then she changed the subject. "Well, I want to get some sleep. I'll see you at school."

"Bye," Left-y said, as she left for the night.

Once he was sure she was gone, he went over to the others. "Did she seem a little strange tonight?"

"No stranger than usual," Rousey said.

"She sounded sad about Sarah," Drummey said. "Maybe she was stressed about that."

"Yeah, she was, but there was something else too. I think she was hiding something."

"What do you think it is?"

"I don't know, Rightey. It could be anything. Maybe she'll tell us later. It's pretty late now. We should go home. After all, it's a school night."

"Don't remind me," Rousey said, as they got their stuff together and set out for home.

September seemed to fly by, and before Left-y knew it, it was the beginning of October. Only a couple of weeks until their big concert in the Urbandome, and The Dangerous Four were practicing harder than ever. They met almost every night for a couple of hours. All of them were getting tired of it, but they could see it paying off. The five of them sounded excellent, and they knew the songs, as well as each other, better than they ever had. It was a particularly cool night when Left-y, Rightey, Rousey, and Drummey were awaiting the arrival of The Jazerae.

"Where is she?" Rousey asked. "Why is she taking so long?"

"Now you know how we felt all those times waiting for you."

"Left-y, I was never that late, was I?"

"Only a few minutes. Let's give her some more time."

"You don't have to wait any longer, Left-y," The Jazerae said as she walked in and got her sax. They had been practicing so much, she just left it in the clubhouse.

"Finally, we've been waiting."

The Jazerae glared at Rousey. "Like you're one to talk."

"At least I'm here on time when it counts."

"Enough of this!" Left-y yelled. "We don't have time to argue. I know we're all tired of practicing this much, but we're almost there. Just another couple weeks, OK?"

"OK," both of them said.

"Good. Now, let's get this practice started."

The practice was not their best one. There were some mess ups and yelling, but they pulled through.

All of them were ready to end the night at 12:30, but Left-y stopped them. "Before we go, I've got something I need to tell you. Mike signed us up to perform Friday night, but he also arranged a publicity stunt for us after the concert."

"What kind of publicity stunt?" Rousey asked. "Are we signing autographs?"

"No, we're going for a bus ride."

"Really?"

"Yes, really. It's for some new bus line, and they wanted us to try out their prototype tour bus. We'll only be on the road for a short time, but it should be a lot of fun."

"I don't know, Left-y," Drummey said. "A prototype?"

"This could be a lot of fun," Rightey said to assure him. "And like Left-y said, we won't be in it for very long."

"OK, if you say so."

"We do."

"Well, you may have to do it without me."

"Why, Jazerae, you don't want to go?"

"No, Left-y, it isn't that. I've got something I need to tell all of you."

They all turned to her and listened.

"Guys, it's been fun, but after our big concert, I have to quit the band."

All four of them just stared at her. Had they heard her right? Did she just say she was quitting?

"What do you mean quit the band?" Left-y asked.

"I have to," she said as she began to quiver. Her voice was shaky and weak. They could tell she was about to cry.

"I've got to go," she said quickly and ran to the door, but Left-y stopped her. He looked directly at her and she looked away.

"Let me go, Left-y!" she yelled as she burst into tears.

"Not until you tell us why. It doesn't make sense, Jazerae. You fought like crazy to get into The Dangerous Four, and now you're just going to walk away? Tell me, what happened?"

"I'm sorry, Left-y. I really want to stay in, but I don't have a choice!" Then she collapsed on the floor.

He knelt down to her. "What you mean you don't have a choice?"

She stopped crying and looked at him. Her eyes were still teary when she answered: "Because I won't be here. My dad's job moves people around a lot. For a while now, he had the possibility of getting a job transfer. Now he has at the end of the month. He's going to a neighboring state; so are my mom and me."

"What are you saying?"

"I'm saying that I'll be moving in about a month."

"To where?"

"I don't even know. Some town like a hundred miles from here. So you see, I have to quit. I really don't have a choice."

All of them were silent. Left-y was stunned. He had known her for so long. Now she was leaving, and there was nothing any of them could do.

"Well, just because you're moving doesn't mean you have to quit," Drummey said, trying to cheer her up. "Maybe you could come back for Christmas or summer vacation …"

"It wouldn't work, Drummey. It's too long of time," Left-y said sadly. He looked at The Jazerae. "I'm so sorry."

"You don't need to apologize. It's nice that you would think of me, but even if we could do it, how long would it last? Really? It seems like no one wants to do this anymore."

Left-y looked up from her to Rightey, then to Rousey, then to Drummey, and back to her. Then he asked the tough question: "Do you guys want to break up?"

"Left-y, I know what you're trying to do, but I don't want you guys to end this because of me."

"It isn't because of you, Jazerae," Rightey said. "We've all been thinking about this for a while."

"But do we want to break up?" Drummey asked.

"We wouldn't have to," Left-y said. "We could take a sabbatical."

"A what?"

"A sabbatical, Rousey—a break for a month or so. We could rest and regroup, figure out what we want to do about The Jazerae leaving."

"That's not a bad idea, Left-y. Maybe we could take a subliminal."

"You mean a sabbatical?"

"Yeah, that thing."

"OK, after the Urbandome, we'll take a sabbatical." Then he looked at The Jazerae. "Will you stay with us until you move?"

The Jazerae looked him straight in the eye and said, "Count on it, Left-y."

"Good. We'll worry about explaining why The Jazerae isn't with us later. It's late, and I'm sleepy. I say we go home."

The others agreed, and they got ready to go.

The Jazerae left the clubhouse and was about to disappear into the night, but Left-y stopped her. "Jazerae?"

"Yes," she said as she turned around.

He went up to her. "No matter where you go or how much time passes, you'll always be one of The Dangerous Four."

"Thanks," she said, as she smiled for the first time that night.

CHAPTER 15

The big night finally came, and The Dangerous Four were in the big city with Mike. A limo was taking them from their hotel to the Urbandome

"Well, there it is," Left-y said, as the limo pulled around the corner, and the Urbandome came into view.

Left-y was a little nervous when he first saw it, but his excitement took over as they got closer. It was getting dark, and the lights were turning on. Everything was so bright. The limo came to a stop, and the chauffeur came around and opened the door. Mike got out first, followed by the others, and then Left-y got out. The first thing he saw were lights, but not from the dome. Instead, they were flashes from cameras. He couldn't see for a few seconds and almost stumbled over his robe, but he got himself together and caught up with the others.

They all stared up at the Urbandome in amazement. There was an electric sign that showed the bands playing that night. One was called Funk34, and then their name came up.

"That's us, wow!" Rightey said.

"I'll say," Rousey agreed. "This place is so, big!"

"It sure is," Mike said, as he nudged them forward. "Go in and have a look around while the instruments are being set up. You will be going on soon, and then you're going on the bus right after, so enjoy the free time while you have it. You've earned it."

"We will," Left-y said, as they made their way in and went down some halls that led to the stage. The curtain was down, and there were crewmen working everywhere setting up their instruments. Left-y couldn't believe the size of the stage. It was huge!

"This seems like a dream," he said out loud.

"I know," Drummey replied. "But it's real."

"I'm so nervous," The Jazerae said. Then she heard something move on the other side of the curtain, and there was the sound of feet stomping, as well as voices murmuring.

"They must have opened the doors and people are coming in," Left-y concluded.

"It won't be long now," Rousey said excitedly.

"No, it won't," Mike said. "I want to wish you guys good luck tonight. Just go out there and have fun."

"We intend to," Left-y replied. As Mike left to talk to some stagehands, Left-y spotted a guy with long, wavy hair dressed in bright colors.

"Check that guy out," he said. "He's got some funky clothes."

"I bet he's the lead singer of Funk34," Drummey said.

"I think I'll say hi," Left-y said, as he walked over to the guy. "Hey there."

The guy glanced at him and then looked away. Left-y tried again.

"I said hey there."

The guy glared at him. "What?"

"I wanted to say hi."

"Well I don't. You guys have made me mad enough tonight."

Left-y was puzzled. "What did we do?"

"We were supposed to go on first. Had the spot booked and everything. Then you punks had to show up and ruin it all. You guys think you're so good. I've heard some of your songs. They're amateur. Better enjoy tonight, kid, because I don't think any of you will be performing here again. None of you have what it takes to make it in the big city."

Left-y was taken aback and a little frightened. "Is this your idea of a threat?" he challenged.

The lead singer laughed. "No, I'm not threatening you. I don't have to. Like I said, this will probably be your only performance here. By the way, you might want to hang around and take notes while we're up. We'll show you how a real band plays," he said as he walked off, leaving Left-y to process what he'd heard. The others came up to him.

"What'd he say?" Rousey asked.

Left-y told them.

"Man, what a jerk!" The Jazerae said. "I've seen Funk34 on TV. They always seemed so nice."

"I guess in show business, not everyone who appears nice actually is," Rightey said.

"And not everyone who appears mean is either," Left-y said as Mike came up to them.

"Are you all right Left-y?" he asked.

"Not really."

"Do you feel like you can't go on?"

"No way, Mike. We've worked way too hard for this; I want to perform," Left-y said, as the audience began to roar with chants. He couldn't make out what they were saying, but it sounded like they wanted some music.

"I think our audience wants us."

"Yes they do, Left-y," Mike said, as he put his hand on Lefty's shoulder. "It's your biggest audience yet—almost twenty thousand people."

"Twenty thousand," Left-y repeated. None of them had been in front of that many people before. It seemed unreal. "Well, we'd better give the people a good show. Let's make some tunes!"

◆   ◆   ◆

The concert went better than they could have hoped for. The roar of the audience was deafening. Rows of people just went on forever. Left-y couldn't even see the end. The sound system was awesome as well. Their music never sounded better. None of them wanted it to end, but the time came, and they took their final bows. Once they were off the stage, and the audience couldn't see them, they jumped around.

"That was awesome!" Rousey yelled.

"That was the coolest concert we've done yet!" Drummey exclaimed.

"Very impressive; you guys rock!" Mike said as he came up to them. "So, you ready for your bus ride?"

"Yeah, let's go!" Left-y yelled. He had to yell because the screams from the audience made it hard to hear.

Mike led them down a few halls and out a side door. The limo was waiting for them.

They all got in and made themselves comfortable. Left-y kept sliding on the leather seats, but he finally got situated. He stared out at the sparkling lights from all the signs and hotels. Then he heard a voice shout: "There's the station, and there's the bus." Rousey pointed out the window. The station came into view, and the limo came to a stop.

"Now here's the plan," Mike said when they were all out. "The bus will leave here and travel to the station back home. I'll be waiting for you there."

"You're not coming with us?"

"No, Jazerae. The tour company only wants The Dangerous Four."

"Sounds good," Left-y said, as they approached the bus, which was a lot bigger close up. It made a low-pitched, powerful rumble that told him it was ready for the road. The door opened, and the driver came down the steps and shook their hands.

"I'll be driving the bus tonight, so if you have any questions, come to me. You guys ready?"

They all nodded.

"Well then, come aboard."

They walked up the steps and into the bus. It was very roomy inside. Unlike the school bus Left-y usually rode, this one didn't have rows of benches. Instead, it began with a narrow hall with beds built into the walls; then it widened in the back to a living room type area with a couch, table, TV, and a small kitchen. There were a few closets around and even a bathroom in back. It looked more like a mobile home than a bus.

"Wow."

"Glad you like it. I'll be up front. It's just the six of us, so feel free to roam around," the bus driver said. Then he walked up to the front of the bus and closed the divider behind him.

A few minutes later, the driver took the brakes off, and the bus began to move.

"This is it," Rousey said. "We're really going."

"Ugh."

"What is it, Left-y?"

"I don't know. I just had a really weird feeling. That's all. Like something wasn't right. It's probably nothing. Forget it."

They did, and soon the bus was on the interstate heading back to their town. Left-y finally got a chance to relax a bit. He had been so excited; he didn't realize how tired he was. "Wow, I'm exhausted."

"We all are," Rightey said. Then he added, "I think we're right in taking a break. As fun and cool as this is, we can't keep doing this. I don't have any free time at all, and I'm getting worn out."

"Yeah, we all are," Left-y agreed. "I'll talk to Mike about a break when we get back," he decided, as he sat down in the booth that made up the kitchen area. He noticed there were seatbelts in the booth. At first, he thought it was funny there were seatbelts in a booth, but he thought about it, and it actually did make sense. So he fastened his. Overall, the ride was pretty smooth, and before they knew it, they could see their town coming up. A few more minutes, and they'd be there.

"You know, this was a cool ride," Drummey said. "I can't believe I was nervous about this."

"Yeah, I don't know why I was either," Left-y said. "I'd ride this bus any day!"

As soon as he said that, the bus wobbled and veered onto the shoulder. The driver made a sharp turn to the left and got back on the road.

"That was close," Rightey said.

The bus veered onto the shoulder again, and the driver hit the breaks.

"I don't think we're done," Rousey said.

Crash!

A sudden force from the rear pushed them all forward. Then the bus began to tilt to the right, and then it fell. All of them screamed and shut their eyes.

Left-y wasn't sure how long his eyes were closed. It could have been a few seconds or several minutes, but when he opened them, he was relieved to see the others were OK. He was leaning sideways somewhat hanging by his seatbelt. He unfastened it and fell.

"Ow."

"You all right?"

"Fine, Jazerae, you?"

"I'm OK. All of us are, except for Rousey, who's whining about his pinched pinky."

"I'm not whining about it," Rousey defended. "It hurts."

"Are you bleeding?" Drummey asked.

"No."

"Then quit whining."

"It's a good thing we had our robes and masks on to shield us from the debris," The Jazerae said. "Otherwise we could have been really hurt, probably cut from the glass."

"Or anything else," Left-y said, as they looked around. All the windows were smashed in. The tables and furniture were broken. The entire inside of the bus was wrecked.

"There's an emergency exit in the ceiling," Drummey said. "We can get out through there."

As they made their way out of the bus and into the ditch on the side of the interstate, Left-y saw a semitruck pulled over, its lights flashing.

"That must have been what hit us from behind," Rightey concluded.

"Oh no!" Rousey yelled.

"Rousey, quit whining about your pinky," Left-y said.

"It's not that. Come to the front of this thing, guys, quick!"

Left-y and the others scrambled to the front to find Rousey staring up at the driver. Rousey was quivering slightly, and Left-y saw why. The bus driver hung limp in his seat, hanging solely by his seatbelt. Blood dripped from his head.

"Is he …" The Jazerae started.

Left-y stepped closer to get a better look. He saw the bus driver's eyes. They were open but blank, as if a mannequin's.

"I think he is."

"That's awful," The Jazerae said. "He died trying to save us."

"I feel sick," Rousey said, and Left-y heard him making gagging noises. He then looked at the lights from their town as Rightey and Drummey walked over to him.

"We almost made it," Drummey said. "We couldn't be more than a half mile from town."

"We need to get going," Rousey said as he had stopped gagging. "We need to get away from this."

"We can't," Left-y said. "We have to wait for the police."

"No, you can wait for them. I'm not staying here," Rousey said as he took off running for the lights.

"I'm with him," Rightey said as he started running too.

Left-y looked at The Jazerae. She shrugged her shoulders.

"I don't want to be here," she said as she started to run. Left-y turned to Drummey.

"You?"

"I think it has to be all of us or none of us."

"Is that really how stuff like this works?"

"I think that's what I heard."

Left-y sighed. "Then I guess it's none of us," he said.

He and the others finished the trip back to their town.

CHAPTER 16

Jake woke up late the following morning still a little dazed. The whole night before seemed somewhat like a dream, and it was hard for him to remember exactly what had happened. He dragged himself out of bed and went down to the kitchen. His dad was reading the newspaper as usual, and his mom and brother were nowhere in sight.

"Morning, Dad," he called. "What's the news today?"

"Well, there was a really bad accident just outside of town last night."

"There was?"

"Here, check it out."

Jake took the paper and read the headline. He couldn't believe what was written.

"It's too bad," his dad said. "But they were kids, and their parents weren't with them. Stuff like this happens when kids live dangerously like that. I'm just glad you're not like that, Jake."

"Yeah," was all Jake could think to say, as a hard knot formed in his stomach. He wanted to look away from the paper, but he couldn't.

"Hey, you hungry? Do you want some cereal?"

"No, I'm good. I have to go," he said as he ran up to his room and called Craig.

"Yeah?" Craig answered in a half yawn.

"Craig, it's me. Have you seen the paper?"

"Why? You missing yours?"

"I'm serious."

"No, I haven't."

"Well check it out. We're meeting tonight."

"But I thought we were taking a subliminal, a substantial, a break thingy?"

"This is urgent. We need to talk. Meet at 11:30!"

"OK."

"I'll call the others, and Craig?"

"Yeah?"

"Don't tell anyone."

Evening came, and the five of them met at the clubhouse. Rousey and The Jazerae were a little annoyed.

"What's this all about, Left-y?" Rousey asked.

"Yeah, why are we here?"

"Have either of you read today's paper?"

They both shook their heads.

Left-y picked up his copy and tossed it at them. "Here's why!"

They both looked at it in disbelief.

"Now do you see why we're here?"

They both nodded.

"Why don't you read it for everyone?" Rightey suggested.

"Here it goes," The Jazerae said. "The headline says, 'The Dangerous Four in a Deadly Crash.'" She let it sink in for a few seconds.

"It says that the tour bus we were on last night suffered 'mechanical failure,' whatever that's supposed to mean; the driver tried to stop but was rear-ended by a semi and couldn't. He was killed at the wheel, but The Dangerous Four were not on the bus. They interviewed Mike; he said no one knows what happened to us, but believes we're OK ... I can't read anymore."

"It's all right, Jazerae. We get the idea."

"Everyone thinks we're OK then?" Rightey asked.

"It said they believed we're OK. This is awful."

"No, it's exactly what we needed!"

"What you talking about?"

"Look, we were going to take a break anyway, and The Jazerae was going to leave. If everyone just thinks we disappeared but are OK, we don't have to worry about The Jazerae. The Dangerous Four are remembered as awesome rock stars cut down too early, and we get our normal lives back. We couldn't be luckier!"

"I don't know. People may be worried about us, and we're fine. Isn't that lying?"

"Not really. We weren't the ones who wrote the article. That's the newspaper's fault. We're just not telling them everything, which is nothing new."

"I guess so, but what about Mike?"

"He'll have to believe it too. No one can know."

All of them thought for a while, and then Left-y spoke: "If no one's got a better idea, we'll have to do it."

He walked over to the table and found a blank sheet of paper. He scribbled something on it. Then he held it up for everyone.

"This is a contract. It states that we all know what happened last night and that none of us are to tell anyone what really happened the night of 'The Deadly Crash' or anything else about The Dangerous Four. If we sign it, it makes it official."

One by one, they all signed the contract. Left-y was the last one to do it. Then he held it up and tore it into five pieces. Each member took one.

"If we are to ever come back to this place or to practice again, all five pieces of the contract must be here."

They all agreed.

"So, this is it," Rightey said. "We're really done now."

"Yeah, we are," Left-y said, as he turned around to look over the clubhouse one last time.

Rousey went over to him.

"You know, Rousey, we never did finish 'Liking You.'"

"No, we didn't, but maybe we will some other time."

"Yeah, some other time."

The five of them walked out and looked at each other one last time. Everyone was fighting the tears.

"Till the next time we meet," Left-y said.

"Till the next time," the others repeated.

Then they all turned and went their separate ways.

As Left-y began to walk away, he spun back around to say good-bye, but he realized it wouldn't do any good. It would be like saying good-bye to someone on the street, some musician, a musician in the night.

THE END

Printed in the United States
by Baker & Taylor Publisher Services